I0673553

CREEK BAIT

STORIES BY

Richard Lutman

CREEK BAIT

LIBRARY OF CONGRESS CATALOGING-IN-PUBLICATION DATA
Creek Bait
Authored by Richard Lutman
ISBN: 9780999461754
LCCN: 2018968034

ACKNOWLEDGEMENTS

Stories in this collection have appeared in the following literary journals: Creek Bait *Prick of the Spindle*; De Nada (de nada *Chiron Review*); The Great Cause (Heroes *Epiphany Review*); Crossing the Great Divide *The Petigru Review*; The Medalist *Verdad*; The Butterfly Lovers *Green Silk Journal*; The Magician *Corner Cupboard Press*; The Stars Are Out In Cabland, *The Bethlehem Writers Roundtable*; Laughter For A Padre (The Laughter of God *Halycon Reader*); A View of Toledo, *Wildflower Muse*; The Blue Lady *The Green Briar Review*; The Calf (Rain Smoke *Literary Yard*); A Pretty Hand (Don't the Governor Write a Pretty Hand *Deep South Magazine*); Birthday Boy (The 13 *Alpha Magazine*).

Dedicated to Jamestown, RI
where these stories
first came to life

Contents

The Butterfly Lovers

Lover, friend, or enemy, for each the attraction to a woman was different; her laughter, voice, eyes, hair, perfume mingled with the night air or the portent of a shape leaning from a darkened doorway. For him, it had been Gloria's high cheekbones, her long black hair, the patch over her right eye, and the way she stood or sat erect with that half a smile on her red lips as if hinting of something she wanted to tell him, but never would. Such simple things to stake his soul on. His stomach knotted as he wondered what lay ahead.

"Gods decide—live or die," she said. "I lover of a Gweilo."

"Don't call me that."

"I call you what want. I have right. You know by now. Stupid. Big stupid."

He sat up and tossed the sheets aside. The dank air of the bungalow felt clammy against his skin.

"No," she said. "Do not go. I want inside me."

"I've loved you enough already."

"Me say when enough."

The legend of the butterfly lovers was wrong. Lightning would never split his grave and set him free as it did for the two butterfly lovers, Ling Shan-po and Chu Ying-tai. As the broken-hearted Ling Shan-po mourned at the tomb of his beloved Chu Ying-tai, a terrible clap of thunder split open the grave, and she joined her lover. The two turned into a pair of butter-flies to fly forever among the flowers.

"Forget butterfly," she said. "Come to Peng Wo. We wear no clothes. Be like when we come into world. Stay in bed all day and suck titties dry."

"The fan has stopped," he said with irritation.

The buildings below the rocky hill were dark.

"Do not care about fan," she said. "Nothing. Some-times I cannot stand sound of you next to me. Get up and run away."

He reached out for his butterfly net and dropped it over her head as she knelt over him.

"You fuck bassid," she said and clawed free from the white netting.

He tossed the net away and stared into the night's oppressive heat.

"Sometimes I forget myself." He shook his head.

"No legend. It happened long ago, in another time. Maybe coincidence. Maybe not."

"Do you love me?" he asked.

"I accept fate."

"Do you love me?"

"It is as my fortune teller says."

Her words made him feel as if he were standing on a crumbling sand bank.

The air of the bungalow was stale with the odors of cigarettes, whiskey and the jungle.

The night sounds made her tremble, and he felt her close and warm against his body, a small comfort ready to tear away at any minute.

Below, the sea was quiet against the rough gray and black granite cliffs. In the photos he'd seen, the other islands of the territory had been visible over the cracked cement wall behind the bungalow. Now green and impenetrable, the brush was a barrier. Rats stirred in the kitchen, then scampered across the floor.

She rolled over and opened his journal, studying the entries written in his careful hand. 'Arrived. Caught 6 butterflies below bridge east of the bungalow: *Erionota torus, Danaus similis, Papilio polytes, Artipe eryx, Euploea mulciber, Danaus genutia.*'

"What name me?"

The pungent scent of midsummer filtered through the screens and hovered about them.

"Something unforgettable so you can tell your children," he said. "You will live forever."

"Better things for children to know."

"Like what?"

"How to please lovers as I please you."

"Will you come with me tomorrow?"

"I go back to Hong Kong."

"I'll go with you."

"Stay, collect butterfly," she said. "I wash your feet before you go."

"I want to be with you."

"You have me now."

"I want to see where you live."

"Nothing to see."

"How do you know?"

"Too interested in me. I crash you down."

"That's my choice. The way you bend your elbow on the railing in the water garden below the bungalow. Your smile. And your smell resembling a fragrant jungle clearing full of flowers…"

She shook her head as if scolding him.

"Not Chu Ying-tai. I Gloria Wong. Gloria, lover of Gweilo butterfly man. Dirty Gloria."

He slapped her.

She turned away, her hair a black screen between them.

"Yes," she said. "Yes. Hit again. Kill Gloria. That best way. Then no Gods."

A night bird broke the silence with a sharp cry, answered by another further down the hill.

"I belong to no one," she said. "Maybe once I loved as in legend and been anything I want."

"It's not too late."

A dog barked from the patio and she sat up, shaking. It peered at them with glowing eyes before it trotted off.

The night breeze rattled the bamboo outside the bungalow.

"Do butterfly sting?" she asked.

"No. They're too beautiful to sting."

"Why you kill?"

"It's my work."

"I sting. You kill me one day?"

"No," he said.

"Even if I hurt?"

"I couldn't."

"Then you same as others. Afraid."

"No. I'm not," he said. "I love you."

"So they."

She stood and paced in front of the screen doors, a luminescent shadow against the night.

The heavy odor of the vegetation reminded him of an unkempt greenhouse. A night bird called again and then fell silent. In the channel, the engine throb of the Macao fast ferry shook the blackness.

"Nights mysterious and full," she said. "Must accept. You die for me?"

"I'd do anything for you."

"Then I hate you," she said.

"Why?"

"Not worth dying for. Dirty. No one want dirty girl."

The pacing stopped, and she was next to him. She laughed, poured out a whiskey, drank, then stood and danced. Her body glistened in the moonlight that fell like a gossamer sheet across the worn linoleum floor.

"See how good," she said. "Me be an actress in a movie. Know how men see me."

She laughed and pushed her hand through her tousled hair.

"People so different," she said. "Tired of faces, bodies, hate voices most of all."

"Do you hate me?"

"Tomorrow new day. See what happens. Things different. Perhaps I love then. Perhaps strong again. Fly away. Never catch. Maybe free of legend. Free of you."

She turned her face to the moon, and her features became hard. A chill shook him.

"I don't want you to leave," he said.

"You have butterflies to catch."

"And at night?"

"Always the night. Perhaps not be back. Perhaps last time."

The words pierced like a shard.

"Nothing more to say," she answered. "Enough already."

"Come back to bed."

"No. Not sleep right now. I keep you awake."

"I don't care."

"Rest for the butterfly. Trail you take dangerous and full of snakes."

"Are you worried about me?"

"I might be."

"Would you mourn me if I died tomorrow on the trail?"

"No."

She fell back on the bed exhausted. He wanted to take her again, to hear her moan against the hot thick night. She laughed and licked his chest.

"How anyone love me again? Not want to be loved that way. Price too high."

As he reached out for her breasts, she tossed her hair over them like a black and fragrant grave.

Creek Bait

THE FILM I'D ALWAYS DREAMED of making about a bait shop would open with the establishing shot of a flat-bottomed boat tied to a dock and herons poised on yellow stilts in the estuary. High tide flooded the marsh. On the wall, hung shiny lead sinkers and hooks of all sizes in plastic packets. On another wall would be a large stuffed fish. At night, headlights from the old highway bounced off the water, and there was a breeze that constantly smelled damp and weedy.

Biggest fish ever caught in these parts, my father would say as I imagined him staring into the camera. Used three-pound test line to bring it in.—Yeah.— Lucky catch. Have a beer.

In reality my brother Howard and I stood in front of a rundown bait shop near Barnegat, New Jersey.

Tape covered a crack in one window; a CLOSED sign was tacked to another. The front end of the faded white building faced the road. A pier jutted out into the tidal creek. A rotting wooden skiff lay in the mud flat behind the shop. I never forgot the thrill I felt as my father snapped the picture of me with my crab net. I stood barefoot in my shorts on a mound of submerged marsh grass. The water was so clear I could see the eyes of the fish head staring at me as the blue claw crab inched up through the water. My father scooped the crab into a net, the still water breaking into tiny waves. The images of the past tormented me. I wanted to get so drunk I could no longer feel anything.

◆

The power lines on the ridge behind my father's house had been where I'd made my first movie: quick cutting images of power lines with opaque water from the narrow stream that ran down the center of the valley where the power lines were. What had I been trying to say? Depict the end of the world? In my bedroom, sheets covered a chair and sofa, and pictures, wrapped in newspaper, leaned against the wall. I searched through the piles of boxes stacked against one side of the room for the reels of film I'd put there. I opened one can, took out the film and held it to the light, then threaded it through the dusty viewer I'd mounted on the desk that had once been my editing table. The film was of my father's first hound running in circles on a deserted beach in New Jersey. I turned the crank faster and faster until the dog's legs were a blur and the end of the film clattered through the viewer.

The camera I'd taken the pictures with had been a 16mm Bolex I'd saved up for. I'd taken it everywhere with me. At that time, the only world that made any sense was what I saw through the lenses of that camera. I had to sell it to help pay for my divorce to Vicky.

◆

It was late summer, one of those leaf-droopy days when I'd first met her. I should have known I would regret that meeting. Her eyes held judgments even then. I was lonely, and she seemed excited when I told her I made movies. When we kissed for the first time she said nothing; she lightly touched my cheeks with the tips of her fingers as if doubting my existence. It was Christmas when I asked her to marry me.

We slipped into an easy acceptance of each other in a way we thought happened only in the movies. We loved being together, and she let me film her. Sometimes she was a clown, a vamp, or a stripper. After three years, she grew tired of my movies and her parts in them and tried to avoid eye contact when we were together. When she asked me if I loved her, I didn't know what to say. That night she turned away. The next morning, she wouldn't look at me.

Sometimes I missed her and the way she held a cigarillo between her two fingers and posed as a streetwalker to get my attention, a pose that became the symbol of the futility of our marriage.

◆

Below me my father stirred on the back porch, and I found him holding a large peanut butter jar that contained a praying mantis on a twig.

"Seven flies," he said with awe. "That's a record for him. The flies have to be alive or he won't eat them."

"Does he eat anything other than flies?" I asked, half curious about its angular green body. Once I'd found a mantis egg sack on a bush and brought it home. The babies hatched, and I remembered how they tickled the skin across the back of my hand until I shook them off. They fell on the floor where they looked like thin green splinters.

"I don't know," he said. "I've never seen him eat anything but flies."

"How big is he going to get?"

"Several inches. I can't let him go yet. It's still young and won't survive. Why don't you make a film about it—some science fiction thing?"

Without waiting for an answer, he pressed his face against the jar. The mantis waved its legs at him.

He put the jar down, opened the lid and shoved in two more flies.

"You didn't stay in Montana long," he said in a judgmental voice.

"I'm going to New York tomorrow. If I find a film job there, I won't go back."

"You can't just do as you please."

I shrugged.

"Look what happened to your marriage."

I turned away and headed into the kitchen which smelled of boiling pasta. I opened the refrigerator and took out two bottles of beer and called Vicky.

The phone rang four times before she answered. When she heard my voice, the line went dead.

I slammed the receiver down and headed outside to clear my thoughts and check out my car, which I'd left at the bottom of the driveway. I opened the door and slid into the front seat, imagining all the highways I'd seen through the windshield on my way to Montana and back. My father stared at me through the car window.

"Where's my beer?" he asked.

I gave him a bottle, opened the car door and stood in the driveway.

"What are you going to do with your car? You can't keep it here forever."

"I won't. I'll give it to Howard. Where is he?—I wanted to see him before I left."

"He didn't come home last night. He's been seeing a girl out near Jenkintown."

"Good for him."

"Her father's a tailor."

"Nothing wrong with that."

"She's a whore."

"How do you know?"

"Her type always is." Beer ran down his chin as he took a long drink from the bottle. "Vicky's getting married."

The news wasn't unexpected. The intimate moments we had shared would now be for someone else. Angry and jealous, I wanted to head to my room and sit in the familiar silence.

Back in the kitchen my father opened a drawer and took out a pair of spaghetti tongs and snapped them in the air, then pulled the spaghetti from the pot and placed it into a strainer.

"How was your trip?" I asked. Every year he took a two-week vacation to places he'd seen in *National Geographic*. This year it was the Pacific.

"Everybody got diarrhea from the food."

"Did you get any good pictures?"

"The ones from the Galapagos Islands were the best. It was hot and lots of tortoises fucking. One climbed up on the other."

The front door slammed and Howard came in, his lips curled into the goofy smile of a stoner. He clattered about in the refrigerator searching for beer.

"Have you ever seen tortoises fuck?" my father asked.

Howard stared at him and laughed.

"Be right back." Our father pushed through the pasta steam, then returned with a slide and a hand viewer. Howard put the slide into the slot. He laughed again and handed me the viewer.

In the center of the picture among some gray rocks were the tortoises. A man in a Hawaiian shirt stood in the background. I wondered how I would have photographed the same scene.

"Who's the guy in the flowered shirt?" I asked.

"A doctor from New Jersey. The heat was too much for his wife, and she didn't go ashore. His name was McIntyre. The fucker could drink."

The sauce bubbled on the stove reminding me of the mud springs I'd seen in Montana.

"Come and get it," said my father. Eat it all. My dogs won't eat spaghetti even if I put meat in it. They'll eat anything *except* spaghetti."

I reached for the tongs and pulled at the quivering mound of pasta draining in the sink, poking at it as if I were a matador dancing about a bull.

◆

The walls of the hotel room on 72nd and Ninth had once been white, but were now cracked and gray. The bureau had a broken leg propped up with a brick. There was one hard wood chair and a small closet next to a basin with sputtering faucets. The bathrooms were down the hall by the pay phone.

If this had been a film, bugs would have crawled across the wall when I woke up half-drunk after a rough night at the Molly B. In the movie, I would drink and feel miserable until I saw a poor girl selling flowers in the street below. She would lift her innocent face toward me and smile saying: Flowers, fresh flowers. Then, seeing her, I'd want to go on living.

But I wasn't in a film. When I woke and staggered to the window, there was nothing but the tail of a dead squirrel fluttering in the street beneath moving tires. A truck blew its horn, and I stumbled to the bureau for the last of the wine I'd bought. I pulled the cork and drank until I could hold no more, making my stomach hurt again.

What if I'd stayed in Montana? It was a strange land full of distances I'd never known before. A country described in a brochure as one of hope, adventure, riches and a place to start again.

I didn't know what to expect as I drove down through the pass into Bozeman toward the university. There were banks, two movie theaters, some stores, then the open land with mountains and more distances I never understood and didn't want to return to. I never questioned why I had been accepted into the university's Film and Television program.

In my last class at Montana State University, Professor Meyer of *Film and TV 101* had leaned against the small desk in front of the room watching us with his sad eyes; a still unlit cigarette hung from his mouth. Two late-comers entered, which gave him a chance to remove the cigarette, crush it out in the ashtray on his desk, then get another. Janet, the blonde from Malta near the Canadian border, wanted to be a producer. Never too friendly with anyone in the class, she sat behind me and fumbled with her glasses. Her perfume made me sneeze. The other was Dale from Ennis, south of Bozeman. He walked with crutches because of a fall from a horse. He'd lost his grip while trying to shoot film of a cow being roped. The resulting footage had been a jerky twisting skyline then dirt. He hunched himself into a seat in the front row and stuck out his plaster cast covered with writing.

"What is editing?" asked Meyer, gazing past us to the studio walls covered in burlap.

"First," he said staring down at his hands then focused back on his class. "It's the process that transforms a miscellaneous collection of badly focused, badly exposed, and badly framed shots containing reverse screen directions, unmatched action, disappearing props, flare, and hairs on the aperture, but not containing close-ups, cut-ins, or cut-aways, into a smooth, coherent, and effective visual statement of the original script for which the director takes full credit. Like God takes credit for your life."

He paused as if waiting for someone to say something. No one did. He removed the unlit cigarette from his mouth and replaced it with another.

He turned to the blackboard and wrote in capital letters:

IMPLICATIONS: PHYSICAL (MECHANICAL)

Again, he faced us.

"This is the handling, splicing, and re-splicing of film," he said. "No creative decisions need to be made. None. Just like fate."

He returned to the board.

CREATIVE: THE CONTINUITY OF THE FILM. HOW IT IS TOLD VISUALLY. COMPILATION FILM. THE JUXTAPOSITION OF IMAGES SHOT AT DIFFERENT TIMES, PLACES AND LOCALES.

The chalk broke and fell to the floor. He took another stick from the trough at the bottom of the board and he continued to write without pausing.

DISTINCTIONS: CUTTER. THE PHYSICAL WORK. NON-CREATIVE.

FOLLOWS THE BLUEPRINT OF THE EDITOR.

THE EDITOR: BOTH CREATIVE AND PHYSICAL.

"Does everyone have this?" he said.

The paper in front of me was blank.

◆

The day after I arrived in New York, I opened the door of the Sterling Employment Agency near Penn Station and stood still for a moment. The room had the musty odor of an old rug. The brown plastic chairs with shiny metal legs were full, and four people were spread out against a narrow counter filling out aqua-colored forms. No one looked up when I entered.

"May I help you?" The receptionist asked. She wore glasses; a glimmer of sweat covered her upper lip.

"I want to fill out an application," I said.

"For what position?"

"The one you advertised."

"Which one was that?"

"For a film editor."

"Oh, that one. Do you have a resume?"

I rested my briefcase on her desk, took out my resume and gave it to her. She took a clipboard from the pile by the phone, scribbled something on a small white card attached to it and handed the whole package back.

"Fill this out and return it. One of our counselors will be with you."

Another man entered and stood behind me. He crunched candy in his mouth.

"Can I help you?" the receptionist asked.

"I'm here about the film editor's job." The man's voice wavered.

"Do you have a resume?"

I headed to the counter. The information was the same as I remembered it, yet my hands still shook and my knees were weak. Name. Date of birth. Phone. Address. Employment history. Dishwasher. Driving a cab. A man came out of one of the employment agency's offices holding a card.

"Bill—," he looked around the room.

A young man with a moustache stood and followed him into a room.

An older woman balancing three cans of film returned the clipboard to the receptionist and leaned against the counter, then shifted her eyes to stare at the others. Another man in a suit stepped out of the door marked 2.

"Tony—"

A bearded man with glasses rose and walked across the room.

I finished filling out the information and placed the clipboard on the receptionist's desk, then returned to rest my elbow on the counter next to the woman and her film cans.

The waiting room was quiet until someone coughed or turned the pages of a magazine. The doors behind the receptionist opened and two men poked their heads around the departing figures.

"Annabelle—"

"Joseph—"

I followed a tall man in a blue shirt and red tie into a small office. I waited for the job counselor to sit before I did. His desk was clean with only a telephone and a small gray metal box full of cards. He scanned my resume and application.

"The editor's job is no longer available," he said. "But I can start you out as an assistant manager at a movie theater on 47th and Broadway. It's a first run house."

I thought of the woman and her film cans and felt like laughing out loud.

"You'd need to be bonded."

"I don't think I am," I said.

"Not much to it."

I studied him as he flipped through the cards. His fingers were fast and sure. He found the card he looked for then raised his head toward me.

"I can arrange for an interview today."

"Sounds good."

He smiled, dialed a number and talked to someone named Bagnall.

"All set. You're to be there at two?" He opened a drawer, took out a form which he filled in and put into an envelope. Through the cellophane window of the envelope were the words, *This is to introduce* .... "Let me know how it goes, will you?"

"I will." I took the envelope, stood and headed for the door.

Once I reached the street, I gazed up at the buildings. The sun rushed to my face.

I remembered that thirty blocks uptown two James Dean films were playing. I'd be in time to make the first show.

◆

The Molly B was a place I'd grown fond of after I moved to New York when I'd stopped there one day between employment agencies. I'd been back many times to have a drink before I went back to my hotel room.

I liked the Molly B because my favorite waitress sensed when I wanted to be alone or when I needed someone to talk to. Sometimes she'd buy me another beer, calling me Mr. Film because I was always perusing the paper for film jobs.

"Any luck today?" she asked.

"Not so far."

The frame, the shot, montage, and the story; the key essentials of filmmaking I'd learned in Montana. Essentials that made little difference in my last interview for someone to film children's birthday parties.

"You'll find something. I read in Cosmo this will be a good month. Let me buy you a beer." She gave me her best smile as she brushed hair away from her face. "Things will work out, you'll see. Do the best you can."

"Is that what *you* do?"

"Yes."

"At least you have a job," I said.

"And a child to raise. That makes it different."

"I didn't know you were married."

"Not anymore, she said. "We had good times together. We lasted six years. He was a machinist before he got laid off. He liked to go to the Bronx Zoo with our son Stephen. On Sundays he'd load us up into his old station wagon and off we'd go to the zoo. He liked to buy yellow popcorn and a bag of peanuts. One day he disappeared, and I never saw him again. I want to bring my child up right, with a family."

"Good for you. What are you doing after work?"

"I have to pick up my son."

"How would you like it if I took you and your son to a bait shop and we could go catch crabs? I never forgot the first crab I caught."

"Bait shop?"

"It'll be fun. I could make a movie about it. You could be my script girl and your son could be me."

"I have to get back to work."

She headed to the table where a young couple sat. They were laughing.

I finished my beer and drifted out into the heat of the afternoon. People hurried by me. I headed as fast as I could to Penn Station and took the next train to the New Jersey shore. It was time for me to scout a location for my film.

I stared out the window of the train and remembered how I struggled with Professor Meyer's final exam. I had wanted to film what was inside me not answer questions.

1. Within a frame draw any image representing still life.
2. Within a frame draw a human figure male or female.

3. Recall a scene from any film or TV show and describe a passage you recall.
4. (Using crayons) Compose colors in an abstract perspective.
5. Draw geometrically three dimensional patterns in various perspectives—as many as you can up to six.
6. Draw an individual shot (recall) of a film or television show which impressed you and state briefly the reasons why you recall it.
7. Draw two shots at the CUT (edit) from a film or television show which impressed you and state briefly the reasons why you recalled it.
8. Draw a shot from a film or television show in which light and shadow conveyed the major impact.
9. Write a short critique about any theatrical film recently seen, discussing script, direction, camera, editing, and acting in technical detail.

The guy I'd caught a ride with left me on the shoulder of a narrow two-lane road across from a bait shop that was nothing like the one from my childhood. It was a small gray building that needed a coat of paint. Flowers sprouted from the rusted frame of a car. An old man sat in a battered boat tied to the end of the dock. The chirping of sandpipers and the slap of water against the pilings soothed me.

I crossed the road and stared down at his weather-beaten face.

"Before I come here," he said in a raspy voice, "I fish with eight tubs for the cods, then down to six.

Four. Then none. My house is neat, yard clean. And the house inside is clean. No man can ask for more. All I want is to get a brown suit I see in the store to be laid out in. Half a mile of line for each tub. Every eight feet a hook, corks to keep the line above the starfish and bottom crawlies. An hour to bait each tub. Two miles of line."

He flipped a cigarette into the water then stood and handed me one of the bait traps in the bottom of the boat, then another. I stacked them on the dock as he nodded at me.

"My customers waited until four a.m. for me to open. I closed for the night only when there wasn't any more business. I loved to talk to the fishermen and never give them a bum steer. I loved it. Loved waiting on the customers.

"We sold bait, that was it. Sold more crabs than anyone in the state, he said. Thirty to forty bushels a week. Sold anything for fishing. If a stranger came in that didn't know where to go fishing, I took him there.

"I used to charge seven dollars a quart for fiddlers. I'd tell them, if you didn't want 'em then I'd sell them to someone else. We were the homeliest bait shop there ever was, opened the least and made the most money. I'd do it all over again. I miss the people."

"How would you like to be in a film about a bait shop? That way you could live forever and never be forgotten?"

"I'd like that. How about helping me with my traps? Then you would know what it's like for your film."

A Pretty Hand

CASS FRANKLIN spent the first few days after his release from prison preparing his charcoal kilns. The work kept him busy, and he had little time to think. Having finished loading the kilns with hardwood, he faced the window with one bony hand holding the curtains apart so he could see the road in front of the house. No one was coming. He needed his wife right now. But she was dead. He'd been unable to see her buried because he'd been in prison. Even though helpless anguish tightened inside him the glow of the kilns through the early morning mist comforted him. He let the curtain drop.

Ducks rasped in the marshes half a mile away. It would be good to go hunting again. Cass remembered the times he and Red Hollander had risen before dawn and gone to their duck blind to wait for the birds. Those were the good days, the days that had meant something.

Footsteps crunched on the hard-packed earth, and he looked through the curtains again to see Red standing in front of the porch with his duck gun in one hand. He was freshly shaven and wore the same faded overalls, blue jacket and crumpled hat that Cass remembered and had missed.

Cass opened the door and stood on the porch, shivering in the chill air as he stared at his friend.

He stepped down the stairs. Red smiled.

"You don't look much different," said Red. "Thought somehow you would."

Cass laughed and shook his friend's hand.

"Where's your truck?" asked Cass.

"Finally fell apart."

"I always told you it would."

"Yeah, I guess you did," said Red. "I thought it would run forever. But it didn't. Just rusted out. Like we're going to do someday."

Red stood for a few moments staring at Cass's house.

"Place looks the same," said Cass. "Everything is just the way I left it. TV even works."

"A bunch of us made sure nothing would happen to it."

"I have whiskey if you want to drink."

"Plumb dry."

The two men headed inside. Red leaned his gun against the wall and took a seat at the table. Cass poured out the whiskey into two glasses, then sat. Red took a drink and made a face.

"What's in this, poison?"

"Just the usual stuff Ike makes. Found a bottle on the steps when I got back here."

Red laughed. "Bet he still uses gasoline to give it that bite."

The shifting patterns of morning light came through the curtains.

"You know something, Cass. I never thought you'd get out. I wasn't sure you'd be set free until the sheriff told me. Even then I couldn't believe it. Came as soon as I could."

Red picked at a piece of straw caught on his sleeve.

"I don't know what happened, Red. I'd still be there but for the pardon. Guess they don't like old men in prison. They let me work the charcoal kilns, was almost like home. Did it for nine years. It didn't make much sense to work on roads or in the machine shop. Besides, making charcoal meant that I didn't have to talk to many people. Think they knew that.

"See this?" He held up a piece of paper then unfolded it. "The pardon from the governor. Signed in his hand.

"'In view of time served over seven years with an excellent record and has been under observation for over five years that he has been cooperative. The Superintendent is of the opinion that he is a prime subject for clemency. A pardon is recommended.'"

He wiped the tears from his eyes. "Wish Becky was here to see this. She believed in me. Didn't know she was dead until the warden told me.

"Before I met her I used to sit for hours on the porch of my place in Preston City, watching the small planes on their approach to the local airport. I could never get over the feeling it gave me. Those pieces of metal landed as if they were ducks onto a pond—some even tipped their wings when they saw me.

"Then one day at Christmas, carolers from across the river came around, and when the singing was over, it was Becky who gave me a poinsettia. She wore a faded print dress with big yellow flowers on it. She wasn't pretty; there was just something about her. She was skinny, too. We found out later that we were both from the same county in southern Georgia."

Red coughed and poured out another round for each of them. He hooked his heels under the chair and sat back.

"Her name was Becky Richmond then," said Cass. "And she missed Georgia as much as I did. Though she'd made a lot of friends, most of them made fun of her ways. Her father had run off to Detroit a few months after she was born and her mama had sent her three brothers to a church school because she wanted them to know God early in life so they wouldn't run off. She had no one favorite when I first met her.

"That was on a Saturday. She came back again the next day. Showed up early. We sat under the trees and talked of trips each of us had taken to Natchez. And how good black-eyed peas tasted when you cook young okra with them in the same kettle.

"Funny how we both knew okra was cooked just enough whenever the peas cracked, and the seeds slipped out. She came back every day after that. Damn, they never told me until it was too late...."

The words choked him.

"You all right?"

"Yeah, I'm all right. It's the whiskey. First I've had since leavin' prison. You never wrote much."

"You know I always had trouble writing letters."

The bouquet of smoldering hardwood from the charcoal kilns drifted past the fences and covered the nearby fields with a fragrant reminder of the past.

"Just like old times," Cass said. "You and me with nothing to do but sit around, waiting for the charcoal, talking, drinking and making ready to shoot the ducks. Still got my old shotgun. Found it where I left it. The only thing my pa ever left me. Don't shoot like it used to, but hell, it's almost as old as I am now."

He picked up an odd-shaped piece of charcoal from the table.

"Feels like balsa. Burn all day. People from out of state used to come to buy it. How about another drink?"

He passed the bottle to Red.

Cass stood and lurched into a back room then returned with a tape recorder.

"Here it is," he said. "Remember when I bought it in Trinity. Took them three weeks to get and cost me over thirty-five dollars. I thought Becky would never forgive me. She got used to it, though. Caught her talking into it once. Nobody interested in it now, except, you, maybe. Those were the good times. Good times. You on your banjo and me sitting with Becky listening, singing when we knew the words."

Cass put the tape recorder on the table, threaded up the tape, plugged it in and turned it on. The recorder reached speed, then the sound of Red singing, high and faltering as he caught the tune, his banjo plunking behind. The reels squealed, and the tape broke. Cass turned it off, sat and studied his hands. It was a habit he'd gotten into in prison. Looking at his hands helped him to think and helped him to forget Tobin, his cellmate.

Tobin had a girl's picture taped to the wall. The girl wasn't pretty. Tobin would lie in his bunk, and smoke cigarettes and stare at the picture. Occasionally he would raise an eyebrow, roll onto his side and knock the ash from the cigarette into a soda can. Then stared at the girl again. He had never met her. She lived somewhere in Ohio and wrote him letters.

The girl had got Tobin's address from the prison priest. Tobin once told Cass that if he ever got out, he wanted him to go with him to meet the girl. The parole never came, and Tobin stopped writing the girl. Several weeks later he was transferred for stabbing a guard, and Cass never saw him again.

He would never forget the defeat he saw in Tobin's eyes.

"How's everyone doing?" asked Cass.

"Pete got married to a gal named Naomi from Webb's Hollow," said Red. "Don't see him much anymore. Guess he's happy."

"And Dan?"

"He got tired of working that land of his, sold out, and went to California. Haven't heard from him in two years."

"What about Ed?

"Killed when his still blew up."

"Good way to go as any."

Two pheasants squawked like an unoiled gate in the trees below the house.

"Anyone said anything?" asked Cass, breaking the silence.

"A fight's a fight, and you beat Dawson good."

"I guess I did. I killed him—judge said it was manslaughter. Dawson never should have called Becky poor white trash."

Cass rose to his feet and took his shotgun from the wall.

"Let's go," he said. "The ducks are waiting. I've been looking forward to this for a long time."

They started toward the marsh where the water was as gray as the clouds above. And later the wind would have a bite to it.

Selecting a place among the tall grass of the marsh they crouched and waited.

Two ducks came in low and fast. They saw the men and became specks on the horizon. Cass and Red watched, scanning the horizon.

Another duck slowed as it prepared to land near them. Cass stood, snapped the shotgun stock to his shoulder. The duck swerved. The shot charge caught the bird square, and it dropped, floundering with a broken wing, and swam randomly.

Cass tried to reach the bird, but it dove to suicide in the weeds. The gray water stilled.

A pair of ducks flew overhead. Both men stood up and fired. A second report smashed and the birds dropped almost on top of them.

"Becky never liked me to hunt," said Cass. "Couldn't understand why I did it. But she got to like duck after a while. Cooked it up really good for the holidays."

Paper-like leaves crackled underfoot as they started back to the house. The charcoal kilns glowed.

Cass took another drink from the bottle he'd brought and laughed, too drunk to stand anymore.

"You all right, Cass?"

"Yeah. I'm all right. Good likker and a couple of ducks. Yeah, I'm fine," he said with a smile.

"Sure?"

"Yeah. And don't the governor write a pretty hand?" said Cass as he took out the pardon.

The Medalist

WHAT HAD HE DONE to deserve such a fate when his future had been before him and Theresa's body waited for him, warm and desirable, in bed? A guitarist with one crooked ugly hand was no use to anyone. He couldn't even pour a drink without spilling it or write his name the way he had done.

He took the medal from his pocket and studied it. The words were visible around the picture of a guitar: FIRST PLACE GUITAR. BANNOCK COUNTRY MUSIC FESTIVAL 1985.

He often wondered why he still kept it and realized it was always good for a story or two and the accompanying whiskeys. He spent his time between drinks riding the freights he used to sing about, not caring anymore where they went. His journey had no end or purpose.

He stood by a shed near the tracks and listened as the eleven o'clock to York raised its voice to the darkness. Night animals answered and distant stars burned in quivering shapes. He hadn't been drunk enough to catch the next freight train. There would be others, and the bar across the tracks looked more inviting. He opened the door, stepped inside, and headed to the first booth. He sat grateful for a moment of steadiness when his body felt almost whole again. The bar wasn't any different from any of the other places he'd seen: a cracked linoleum floor and the same sour beer and cigarette smell mingled with perfume and sweat.

"What would you like?" the waitress asked, as she came to the booth where he sat. "We have something for everyone."

She was tall, her black hair tied back with a thin piece of polka dot cloth. Her smile was friendly, and it made him feel as though he knew her and had always wanted to know her.

"Kentucky Straight Bourbon on the rocks."

He turned to watch her legs as she moved away. She returned with his drink and placed it on the table.

"Haven't seen you around before."

"First time."

"I hope you like it here."

Her second smile had been inviting and a little wistful, something he hadn't expected. He studied her as she stood before him. In the dim light, she reminded him of Theresa.

Theresa had been there when he won the medal for guitar playing at Bannock five years ago when his future looked good. She wore her hair straight, but because she liked to twist it on top of her head, she looked like a little girl playing at being old. They'd gone to Three Forks to celebrate in the all-night bars. He drank too much, stumbled and put his playing hand through a glass door. He never found out where Theresa had gone.

He stared at his hands.

"Are you all right? Is something wrong?"

What the hell, he thought to himself. He wasn't one to hide his thoughts. Besides, it made no difference. He'd be gone soon.

"You remind me of someone named Theresa."

"I always remind people of someone else," she said with a smile.

He met her eyes. They held a look of understanding, a look he remembered Theresa never had. He didn't want her to go away, not yet.

"I was a good guitar player."

"I'm sure you were."

"Like pro good. That good."

"You don't have to convince me."

He'd said too much and sensed she knew it, but it made no difference. He fell silent and stared at the bartender who was reading a newspaper as though he had all the time in the world for such things.

"How about buying me some gum?" she asked.

He reached into his pocket feeling coins in his hand.

"Here," he said, giving her four quarters. "Buy a lot of gum."

"Want some? It's no fun chewing alone."

He smiled.

"That's more like it," she said. "That's better."

He watched her at the gum machine. She shifted the weight of her body from hip to hip knowing he was watching.

She came back and sat. He was forgetting Theresa and all the trains he'd rode.

"How about walking me home? One never knows what might happen in this part of town."

It had rained, and the streets glistened. As a child, rain had made him think of funerals; figures in damp clothes huddled around a mud-filled hole. Why were people always buried in the rain? Did the rain make them grow, rejuvenated like seeds? Once, he'd held his twisted hand out into the cold drops, but nothing happened and the drops slid off his skin.

The waitress' place was a small two room apartment that smelled of jasmine. On one wall was a large mirror with postcards stuck along the edges. One card showed an ocean with palm trees, another was of mountains, and a third of trees covered in snow.

"I like collecting them," she said. "I've already filled a shoe box. Sometimes I look at the pictures and imagine myself there. It's not such a bad thing. Don't you have any dreams?"

"I did once. Good dreams."

"I know they were. You should never give up dreaming. How can you live without a dream?"

He wished she would stop talking, but knew it was impossible.

Soon she lay next to him in bed, and he felt good, better than he had in a long time.

"I don't know," she said after gazing at him for a moment and smiling an attractive lopsided smile.

"I liked you when I first saw you come through the door. But there was something else. I think I wanted to help you. You seemed as if you needed help. I've always been a sucker for things like that."

He had no answer, letting the spell continue.

"I didn't know what you thought of me."

He lifted his head and rested it on the heel of his hand looking at her face. Her bar smell was strong and addictive. It would be so easy to leave; he'd done it before and found another bar with another girl. He couldn't bring himself to do it, not now at least, the moment wasn't right.

The yellow glow of the street lights illuminated her bedroom. The same glow that lit the finger bone of a saint which had been on display at a church near the center of a town he'd passed through where a big advertisement in the paper next to the used car section announced the viewing times. The church had been full of people waiting to see the relic. He'd gone in very early and walked down the aisle in profound silence. A small piece of discolored bone lay on piece of plaster under a glass case. The texture and shape were the same as a weather-beaten piece of wood. A woman next to him had knelt, her face swollen with a tumor, asked for forgiveness. In desperation, he'd also prayed to be whole once more.

The waitress laughed, looping her arms around his neck and held him. He felt his heart beat with hers. She made him unsure of himself.

"What are you thinking?" she asked in a quiet voice.

He studied her, trying to find himself in her eyes. The image he saw made him feel like crying. He looked like an old man.

"Talk," she said. "Talk to me." Her voice had a frightened tone as she studied his hard, drawn face.

For a moment he didn't feel like responding. "Would I have liked you as a child?"

"I think so," she said with a laugh. "What a thing to say. My mother always said people liked me. She and my father were killed in an accident outside Chicago; a truck full of bibles hit their car."

He touched her lips, trying to make her stop. He didn't want to become that part of her life right now. It wouldn't be fair.

"Please, "she said. "I want to tell you. I was seven. I went to live with my aunt and uncle. They had a small store outside of a small town on the Illinois plains. I left there when I was seventeen. There's not much else. I took a job in a restaurant until one day this guy came in. He talked like they all did; said he'd come from a small town much like the place I'd came from. Said he'd made money and would see the big city. He was friendly and had a nice smile. I thought he was different than the others until he left me."

Tears shone in her eyes, but she didn't cry. He didn't know what to do and held her. He needed a drink, then he would be all right and sure of himself, just like the day he'd won the medal and the world was his for the taking.

She trembled. He reached out and touched her breasts. Her face. Her hair. Her eyes. He held his crooked hand toward the moonlight. It no longer felt connected to him, sparkling and silver in the light.

"Play for me," she said. "Play for me."

He took the imaginary guitar. His fingers brushed the frets. Tears wet her cheeks.

"Tomorrow," he said. "Let's get out of here. We can find a car and drive up into the hills, then just sit back and listen to the radio, getting drunk, not worrying about anything. It will be like it was."

"Yes," she said. "It will be. But you'll have me now and not Theresa."

He stared at her breasts, then looked away, not wanting her so soon. She took his ruined hand, kissed it then placed it between her legs.

The Great Cause

M Y NAME IS MILLER, Corporal Thomas W. Miller, II. I'm the only one left to search and destroy. The orders were clear. I must follow them. The others are dead or have deserted. We had been promised a hero's welcome and much family honor when we returned from the front, but that was months ago. I write these words because of the futility of the act. Who will read them when I'm gone?

About half-past someone broke into the last of the storerooms. Several pairs of children's shoes were stolen. The tracks I followed led toward the sea. I turned back as the weather worsened.

The cold black rain, characteristic of this place, has ended. Magnificent white birds driven from the mountains swoop down screeching as they dive. In earlier times, stories were told of how the birds came to take the unguarded babies from the poor. Because of the rain, I must be careful what I touch.

Today I stuff the cracks around the iron door of the bunker with strips I tear from my blanket. The strips do little against the wind, but it gives me something to do. Large clouds hide the moon. I miss the nights when it was so bright you felt the moon burn your face. I remember as a child I lived in fear of being scarred by the silver light. My wife cried when I told her and then cradled my head in her arms, telling me not to fear anymore because she was there to protect me. I look at the words I've written to her:

My Dear Wife:

I remember so much. In this godforsaken bunker, my mind's eye conjures you, my Anne. It is cold, and hard to put my thoughts to paper. My hands are sore. I remember your lovely face. Your brown hair; the way you talked and whispered of your love, the fullness of your lips, the deepness of your eyes, your laughter. My dearest.

When I first heard my name from her lips, the sound of it startled me and not what I imagined. It was like music. She laughed in that soft way of hers and then took off her clothes and waited for me in the bedroom full of shadow and her musky smell.

I put the letter with the others I've written.

Near midnight I hear laughter and voices of children. My search for them locates nothing.

There is a pain in my chest when I cough—an old ailment. I lied about my condition so I could join the Great Cause and become a hero. I felt jealousy toward the retired soldiers who told their stories of war as they sat under colored balloons and wore newspaper hats, their chests full of medals.

When the conflict broke out, my unit was shipped to the northern border. Like so many others, my wife went east to work in the factories. It was war, and everyone had to do their part for the Cause. I never heard from her again.

Early one evening after the sun had set and the smell of yellow blossoms still saturated the fresh air, a series of explosions shook the capital. The day I left, the sky was filled with a vast disorder of flying shapes.

More canned food, water in a red carton and a small broken mirror. I stare at my half face in wonderment and don't remember looking like this. Perhaps I no longer exist.

At about four, a fire spread below the hill. I stand as close as I dare to the flames for warmth.

The fire extends far to the west; mountains of smoke block out the yellow sky. It is difficult to assess the damage. Hundreds of rats run to safety. Using a large stick, I kill two dozen of them in less than half an hour. This is the most exercise I've had in several days. I remember the soft black eyes of one as it stopped, rose, held its paws together, and then raced forward once more.

The fire burns itself out leaving piles of smoldering rubble and windblown cinders. Water pools give off scalding steam from the hot bricks of the ruined buildings. The air is thick with smoke, and it is hard to breathe. In my search, I discover a book of fractions, untouched by the flames. I study it as I sit cramped on the pieces of wood that serve as my bed and chair. If I read ten pages a day, it will take me half the year to finish.

The sun is out, and I go below the hill to better assess the damage. Little is left from the fire, but I collect what I can salvage: a hat, a pair of glasses and more canned food which I save. I stumble into a shell crater and bruise my leg. Much coughing from the smoke. The damage to this part of town is severe and complete.

My leg has swollen above the ankle, an ugly purple with yellow at the edges. It is difficult to move. Great pain. The skin is black above the shin bone. As soon as I am able, I know I must go to the sea where I think the children are.

I hear noises in the street throughout the night, tin cans being thrown, children's shouts and an occasional shot. It is as if whoever is there knows I cannot move. I fashion a crutch from a piece of wood and search once more. There are footprints and several broken cartons strewn over the ground. Many have bullet holes through them, and more windows are shattered. I cannot do much because of my ankle.

A helicopter roars overhead heading east. Before I can ready myself to signal, it's gone. Smoke still lingers.

The swelling is down and I am able to extend my search of the fire area. I discover a picture of a man and a woman. It is a quiet moment. The room in which I discover the picture smells of decay. There are many dead rats on the floor. A coat has been left in a pile against the wall; it is much too large and covered with mold. I find this letter in the coat's pocket. Am I the one meant to read these words?

There will be a ball here next Friday night, and I want you and Charley the Captain to come. They say they will have a good time, and I want to ask Harry if he will lend me his jacket and belt. Tell him I will take care of them and should like it very much if he will lend them, and I will go out to the depot and pick up the jacket and belt. Just write me a line if you are coming. If you do, I will meet you at the depot next Friday night. Just send me a line before next Wednesday so I can get it that night and very much oblige. I talked of coming down next Saturday so goodbye for this time. And I remain your old chum.

P.S. send the letter to the post office. I wish I had a title to my name. It is raining like the devil now. So farewell—you must not get married until I do.

I tear the letter into pieces and step outside and toss the bits into the air.

The black rain returns. Everything is wet and gray. My breath condenses into smoke against the cold. I discover a large green beetle crawling on the dirt floor and put it in a jar I've been saving.

The wild irregular rain continues. Much coughing. Ankle still sore and the roof leaks where I hadn't expected. I share my meal with a beetle. He pokes at my offering with his claws. I patch the leaks as best I can, but the floor is soaked, and I am uncomfortable. Everything is damp. I clean my rifle again and check on my ammunition. It is dry and ready for use.

It is cold this morning, and I sit with the door shut tight. I tear out the pages of the fraction book to start the fire. It is hot and stifling. The beetle died overnight, and I burn him—he sputters in the flames of my stove and disappears.

I rise early to check the traps I've set out for the rats, another pair has been trapped, and they are smaller than the last ones. I smash my fingers resetting a trap. Soon they will be all that's left to eat.

Rained hard again last night. It is damp and cloudy once again with much mud. I follow more tracks leading to the sea. They are fresh and made with new shoes. I can still make out the lettering on the soles, but I lose the footprints among the rocks.

Snow starts toward midnight. How eerie to watch it despite the worsening weather… A restless night. I awake sweating.

Helicopters, this time far to the south. The fingers of my right hand have become swollen and discolored. I'm afraid of diseases. In the anatomical museum near where I lived were the untreated results of diseases preserved in jars that lined the shelves in the basement storeroom.

The storm ends. The snow has drifted hard. Did anyone else watch the snow blown like diamond dust through the white winter's light? The weather clears toward dawn and I head out to search for more coal and find enough in an old furnace bin to fill my bucket. The air hurts my lungs. The swelling in my fingers has lessened.

Clear and cold. A helicopter again in the night. There is much shooting and rocket fire below the hill. From the open door, I see many explosions—bruises in the dark.

My coal is low again and my water supply has frozen—I chip the ice out and thaw it next to the stove. Coughed all night. More snow.

The wind is blowing very hard making travel difficult. I need more coal. Traces of footprints again toward the sea. Many craters and pieces of frozen bodies make identification impossible.

I walk into the woods and hear no birds, only the cold chatter of a half-frozen brook. When I scrape away the snow, the ice is shiny. Weather clearing at last.

I think tonight is Christmas Eve, and I am strong enough to head to the sea. I reach the dunes by midday. A strong and bitter wind blows, and the air is full of stinging spray. Metal wrecks are everywhere with many broken dials and scattered helmets. I feel as though I am being watched. There are more footprints, remains of fire, fish bones, and clam shells. I follow fresh tracks along the beach past the hollow gray rollers with wind-tossed crests. I come to the edge of a large dune—below me on a patch of sand protected by thorn bushes are the children. They do not see me. Several of them are kneeling. The others stare at me. In their center are two cloaked figures.

One of the figures suckles a small baby. The man beside her has a beard and he studies me with his great sad eyes. I go halfway down the dune and stop, rifle raised and ready.

"Who are you?" I say. "Who?"

He does not answer.

"What are you doing here?"

He turns and walks away. The children follow.

"Stop or I'll shoot."

He continues to walk.

"Please," I say again. "Please."

I open fire.

Several of the children stop, turn and aim their rifles at me. The first bullet goes deep into my chest. All is quiet. My name is Miller. Corporal Thomas W. Miller, II. I'll miss the chirping of robins and the squirrels chasing each other up and down and around the tree trunks of my home.

The Magician

Today I saw a magician die. Maybe it was my luck to be in the wrong place again. That's how I got this crooked scar on my face from a jealous lover who thought I cheated on him. If the two men with him had come in five minutes later, I'd have been upstairs with Lucas, none of this would have happened, and I'd still be at Berenson's Social Club with the other prostitutes looking for a better life.

The body of the wizened magician sagged between the two men who carried him. One was a tall clown with a long bent silver hat, the other a stocky curly-headed man in shirt sleeves. I couldn't tell how old the clown was; his pale face and piercing gray eyes made me uneasy. I heard myself say hurry, drop him somewhere and leave.

Right away I knew something wasn't right because nobody like those two would come in here unless it was necessary. They appeared to be respectable. I could tell Lucas didn't like them barging in. His eyes narrowed and his jaw tightened. He wasn't one for being disturbed when he was having a good time. I'd heard there were more than a few who'd regretted bothering him. He finished his whiskey and studied the men.

The two stood for a moment as if they weren't sure of where they were, and half a dozen of Berenson's women dressed in their shear pink, blue, and yellow robes pushed close to stare as if they had nothing better to do. Berenson wouldn't like that. You could bet on it.

"We need a place to lay him down," said the man in shirt sleeves. "Hurry."

Berenson swore and plowed forward with that way she had as if she was someone important, which she wasn't. I can tell you that.

She shoved the women aside with a quick hard tap from that damn ebony cane of hers and studied the three men. The shiny red dress she wore hung from her thin body. An old tattoo smudged her left arm.

"What do you want?" she banged her cane on the floor. "I own this place. You can't come in here like this. Who do you think you are?"

"I have a show to finish," said the man in shirt sleeves. "I can't leave him out by the wagon. I'm Sieble, the manager. I must get back. There's another show."

"I don't care about your show. Put him in the next room on the sofa and get out quick. You're bad for business."

Sieble reached into his pocket and flipped a coin to her. She caught it before it hit the floor and then eyed it as if it smelled bad. Just like her.

"Is that all you have?"

Sieble glared at her and gave her another coin.

She put the coins into a small purse and snapped it shut.

"I warn you. I don't need any trouble. I have friends…. This way."

She headed into a side room, fumbled in the dark, and lit a lamp. I'd been in there once before with a special gentleman. The walls were covered in a dusty smelling ornate purple brocade. A large mirror hung from the back wall. A bottle of Berenson's best whiskey was on a small table near the door. I remembered the man I'd been with that night smelled of peppermints and liked being tickled with yellow feathers. When the night was over, he'd gone upstairs with Berenson, and I'd lost out on my cut.

"Make sure you take his shoes off," she said. "I don't want to get anything dirty."

She slid a pillow under his head, shook out a blanket and draped it over his body. "Just as long as he doesn't die. I run a good place, you understand."

"He'll be all right," said Sieble. "He needs to lie down. That's all. You can't let him die. He owes me money."

"I don't care," Berenson said sharply.

I'd gone back to Lucas because he'd paid for a dance, which meant I'd get extra money when the night was over if Berenson didn't get it first. Even with my scar on my face, he said I was the most beautiful woman he'd seen. I knew he was lying, but the words made me feel good, and I liked the attention he gave me.

"I want you to look after the gentleman in the other room until his friends get back," she said. "I'll take care of Mr. Lucas."

He blew smoke into the air, smiled and kissed my hand.

"If you don't like it you know what you can do," Berenson said.

I knew what I'd like to do to her, but I'd had those thoughts before.

Lucas shrugged, poured out a drink and held it toward Berenson.

"We'll come back later after the show is over," said Sieble. "It won't be long."

"It better not be or I'll charge you a hundred dollars extra."

I took my time reaching the room where the magician lay

"He collapsed," said Sieble. "He was doing a magic trick. It wasn't a difficult trick—he'd done it before. I knew he was sick. Ever since we left Marquette something wasn't right. But this…. What am I to do? He's been with us a long time now. And the people like him. If he dies, I don't know what will happen."

"You should have seen the tricks he could do," said the clown. "But there was so much more. They're things he did that couldn't be understood.…"

"Maybe he'll make himself well again," I said. "Then I can go back out front where I belong and your show will go on as if nothing happened."

They nodded and elbowed their way through the women and their partners to reach the darkened street.

A large gold watch slipped from the magician's vest pocket, and I reached for it. Inside was a picture of a girl, her youthful face highlighted by a smile above a high collar secured by a clasp. I thought about taking it and felt something inside tell me no.

I studied the image. The face of the girl looked like the magician, only much younger and fairer. I closed the cover, wishing he'd been sick somewhere else. I cursed him, which didn't make me feel better. His strange cinnamon smell choked me, something else I cursed him for; then I slid the watch back.

He tried to rise and fell back on the sofa.

"It's all right, old man," I said. "It's all right. Lie back now, take it easy."

"Where am I?"

"Berenson's. You collapsed in the street."

He smiled and shook his head.

"As good a place as any, I guess. Don't you think?"

"I don't want anything to happen," I said with anxiety.

"Everything will be fine. You'll see."

"I wish you could do more than that."

"Perhaps I can," he said.

His eyes held mine until I turned away.

"What's your name?"

"Portland."

He smiled. "You were named well. I have cousins named Florida and Georgia. And I met a lady once called Montana, Lottie Montana, the most beautiful of them all. You look like her. I am the Great Octavius, Master of Magic and all that is Magic."

He reached into the air, turned his hand about, and pulled a coin from his fingers, then he gave it to me.

"That's the easiest way I've ever seen to get money," I said in spite of myself. He chuckled, and thumped the hat against his legs, flipped it upright and drew out a bouquet of yellow roses, luminous and fragile in the dim light. He held them toward me.

"Magic is real; that was just a trick. There's still much that needs to be done where you are concerned."

"What do you mean?"

"You'll see. Everyone will. But I need a drink to clear my head."

I poured out a glass of whiskey and gave it to him. He took a drink then offered me the glass. I took it and drank, wiping my lips with the tip of my tongue in the way I knew men liked. He gazed at me as if he knew what I'd do and smiled. The whiskey made me feel strange and lightheaded.

"My hands used to get raw in the winter, so raw they would break open and bleed. I unloaded freight cars and slept in a chicken coop next to a hotel. The chickens would wake me early. No one believed in what I could do. What was magic to them the sleight of hand, a disappearing coin, and a forgotten name recalled?

"Years later I played in San Francisco and received top billing. I went back to the place I unloaded freight cars, but the railroad had closed down and no one remembered me. There isn't any real magic left anymore, not the kind that means anything. Do you understand? It's all illusion and fakery."

I shook my head, not wanting him to go on. Why was it that men wanted to tell me about themselves? I didn't ask for it. Was it my scar they felt sorry for? I turned away, poured another drink and downed it.

He sat up holding a short chewed-up pencil and took a piece of paper from his coat. Using his hat as a brace, he began to draw.

"I was paid one hundred dollars to draw Lottie Montana," he said, studying me with an intensity that was uncomfortable. "Not only was she beautiful, she was also a singer of the finest rank. We were on the same program. Lottie Montana in blue with a necklace of African diamonds around her neck. Afterward, she sent me her card. I saw her one time after that, but she was too busy and didn't see me. I heard she went to Europe. I wish I could have gone with her. The magic we could have performed would have had all of Europe at our fingertips. But I couldn't leave my daughter. And now...."

He unhooked the watch from his vest.

"Will you give this to my daughter?"

He handed it to me. It ticked against my palm.

"Sieble knows how to reach her."

He put down the piece of paper, checked his hat, rose to his feet, and stepped to the center of the room.

"What are you doing?" I asked. "You're meant to lie down."

"I can't," he said. "Not now. It's time for me to help you."

"I don't need any help," I didn't want to argue. "Not from you."

I took hold of his arms, but he was a lot stronger than I thought. He shook me off and opened the door to the next room. The sudden silence of the other room frightened me.

"I am the Great Octavius at your service," he said bowing. "With your permission, we shall begin."

He reached into his hat and removed a dove which he held for everyone to see. He opened his hands, and the dove lingered in the air and tilted toward the ceiling.

Lucas drew his pistol and fired. The bird tumbled to the floor, feathers suspended in the air behind it. The women let out frightened exclamations and moved back into the shadows of the room.

"That's enough." Berenson pounded her cane against the floor. "Enough. I run a good place. Do you hear? I want you out of here now."

The magician lurched forward and picked up the shattered body. He cupped his hands and held them toward the ceiling again. When they opened, a dove fluttered upward, circled the room, and landed on his shoulder. He caught Lucas's eyes, winked, cupped his hands and let another dove flutter into the room, then bowed, gasped, clutched his chest, groped his way forward, and pitched to the floor. He tried to rise, shook his head and fell still.

Berenson bulled through the excited circle of women and stood looking at me where I knelt over the body.

"I told you to watch him. Can't you do what I tell you?"

"He was dead when they brought him in here," I said with a harsh laugh. "Didn't you know that?"

"Know it all, do you? I'll take care of you later. Now get him out of here."

The room smelled of gunpowder and sweat.

The magician's hat came to rest against the wall then toppled over, filling the room with birds and feathers. Some women tried to catch the feathers; others swept them away with their hands. A dove landed on the chandelier and cooed.

I looked at the flowers Octavius had given me and then at the picture he'd drawn. It was my likeness. A halo and shawl covered my head. I tried to laugh and crumpled the paper into a tight ball. I threw the ball to the floor, poured out a drink and downed it, knowing it would do no good. Nothing would. I opened my hand and stared at the watch.

"What's that?" said Berenson. "Are you holding out on me? Remember the last time that happened, don't you?"

The smell of cinnamon filled my mouth and burned my eyes, and I turned to look at the body of the magician whose gloved hand pointed toward the street. I froze for a moment, then came an imperceptible tug on my arm.

"Where are you going?" said Berenson as she tried to block me. "You can't walk out on me now. No one does. You'll be sorry. I'll see you never work again. Do you hear?"

The night was full of stars. I stood gazing at them, feeling feverish and excited, and headed down the street to Sieble and his wagon where I thought I saw a dove flutter in the cool night air.

De Nada

SOMETHING WOULD HAPPEN TONIGHT, he was sure of that. Even in his drunken state, the soft night tugged at him in a way it hadn't in the past. He shook his head to clear it, finished the bottle of gin, and shattered it against the wall of his room.

Since arriving at Cristos on the San Paulo peninsula three years ago, he drank. It had become his only consolation and made him forget that he was still *de nada*, an alien to the thick green jungle he wanted to be part of. He closed his eyes. The moon pressed on his lids and the night's heat beat down on him. Bats hanging from the eaves shifted their toes and dropped bird bones onto the plaza below.

After selling his interest in his tobacco shop to his partner it hadn't taken him long to decide where he wanted to go. Cristos was the paradise he had dreamed about, a country of rich, flowery trees, spicy scents, herons, eagles, butterflies, and the gray-eyed gypsy. She'd lain next to him on the cool white sheets stroking his chest with her silky fingers.

"Nothing will be the same after tonight," she had said. "Can you forgive me for what I've done?"

"I don't understand," he'd answered. "There's nothing to forgive."

"Someday you will. By then it will be too late."

"What do you mean?"

"That's all I can tell you for now."

"Will I ever see you again?"

"Perhaps."

She rose, and he followed her to the edge of the jungle. She turned to face him in the swirling mist, then was gone. The smell of gardenias closed around him. The jungle still excited him in the early morning. The shafts of sun and vapor through the trees looked like the start of a new world, waiting to be discovered. A light breeze had rippled the tourmaline sea in front of his hotel. He stared into the dark and thought of the other times he'd lay in his hammock hearing the stir of birds waiting for the gypsy to return and couldn't fall asleep until dawn came.

◆

The cry of a night bird in the bushes below his hotel room startled him. The moon disappeared behind a ragged cloud. He let the hammock fall still and listened to the distant rumble of the sea, the shifting of the leaves and smelled the unpleasant scent of blossoms. Small animals called from the trees and alleys, and the sound of a coffin being moved grated against the stone angels and cupids in the narrow alley next to the hotel.

He rose and walked back into his stuffy rooms, headed toward the stairs and down to his battered truck. He had to find something to make his blood flow, to nullify the gin, the night sounds, the moon, and his thoughts.

It wasn't a difficult drive. He'd done it before, streaking through the dark at seventy or eighty, slamming the gears and speeding up on curves. Soon his brain cleared, washed out in danger.

The headlights caught a moth, then he felt the jolt of his truck as it struck a possum-like animal. Looking back, he saw the body drag itself from the road. He put the pedal to the floor and roared down the hill to the village.

For a moment he sat in his truck outside the Morado Ángel. The night boats rocked in the harbor before him. The faces of the fishermen were indistinct, with only the movement of their bodies visible. Gulls, clustered in the beam of his headlights, merged with the flickering crystals of water. He shut the engine off, lit a cigarette, and ragged blue smoke swirled around his head.

He climbed out of his truck, breathed, and took a step toward the bar. The door to the terrace was open to the warm night, and he went in. It was a large room with a dull wooden floor and jukebox. Adjusting to the interior, he sat facing the empty terrace where tables stood in the shadows of the leaves.

He smelled gardenias and lifted his eyes to the figure at the bar. His body stirred with the brassy rush of the fear he sought. Her gray eyes highlighted an oval face. On her throat, she wore a small green stone that pulsed in the light.

Music from the jukebox spilled out into the room. The cook scooped peppers onto a plate filled with a large slab of meat. A man in a tuxedo leaned against the heavy wooden bar and gave her a brown packet she hid it in the folds of her thin cotton cloak, then he disappeared into the night. He caught her eye and saw a faint smile on her face.

A stoop-shouldered woman with frizzy hair swept at the flies that buzzed over her sleeping baby who lay on the table. Behind her a man was lost in pinball.

"Do you have any gin?" he said as the gray-eyed woman approached.

She nodded.

"Bring me a bottle."'

A baby-faced sailor stood and danced with himself. He stopped as the music died and counted his money in the steady blue light of the jukebox, his face grotesque and dark. He shouted in broken German and disappeared into the night, singing.

She returned with the bottle.

"Stay. Have a gin with me."

"I can't, but give me something for the jukebox. I want to hear music."

He gave her a coin and watched her go to the machine, select a record, and sway to the music, eyes shut. The song ended, and she came to him, face glimmered with sweat.

"Sometimes I wish I could dance forever. Don't you? If I could keep things away for a little while. Perhaps…. But that is too much for anyone to ask, even for me."

He followed her outside. The night air was damp and clung to him. She turned into a side street and climbed a set of wooden stairs. A large black spider slid into a crack in the stone wall above him.

She opened the door into her dark pungent room and turned on a small lamp. On a table was a loaf of bread covered by a plastic dome, a wine bottle and a large bible.

She sat on the edge of her bed, bent her arm, and gasped. The needle glimmered in her hands and she offered it to him. He took it, filled it, and tightened the surgical tube on his upper arm, feeling the veins bulge. He slid the needle in, hot against his skin, and felt it drain, then withdrew it in a spurt of blood.

A giant ship in the harbor let out a cry, and he heard her voice singing.

"Little One,
Oh, Little One
So deep enchanted, beauty bound
So caught with love of thee
I cannot part the draught I've found
From thy great hold on me
Little One, Oh Little One."

He took a deep breath. The drug devoured his bones and made them ache and burn. He smelled hot wax and damp stone. His body glided its way along a vista of color. He reached his hands out, and the light tumbled about him.

"I'm called Margaret, with one 'E'," she said in a voice that sounded far away. "I tried to kill myself once by walking into the water. It was grand. The water closed around me. I thought I was in my mother's womb."

She grabbed his hand and held it as if trying to keep her balance. Up close she smelled of dried flowers and old lace. Her face was delicate and cool like a piece of white porcelain. In the silence, he heard her excited breathing.

She lit a candle and started for the door. He followed her outside through the night sounds, and damp scents of the jungle.

How beautiful the jungle became, column after column of trees in a vast hall. He felt the cold stone of the brush-covered wall that ran alongside them. In the flame of the candle, he saw that each stone showed a station of the cross, covered by gray moss. A mugginess hung over him, characteristic of jungles at night.

The candle sputtered out. Darkness and grass brushed their arms. Then they burst onto a moonlit beach. Silver tinted waves rolled ashore. She stopped and examined his face; her eyes glowed.

"My first lover was a sailor," she said. "The muscles of his body were tight and hard. The Indian Ocean was his favorite place. Once, we went to a deserted beach to spread the ashes of a friend over the waves. On the beach were hundreds of stranded jellyfish, baked hard in the sun, and a couple making love, oblivious to our presence. We dreamed of returning. One day my lover drowned swimming to a reef. It wasn't very far, and the tide was low. It was a night just like now…. He gave me this." She took the green colored stone from around her neck and held it, her eyes febrile and alive with expectation.

She swayed back and forth on a small patch of sand, laughed and knelt by a dark tidal pool, tracing circles in the waterfall of the reflection of the moon.

"I want to die like the sperm whale," she said, "who even in the flurry of death always keeps his head toward the sun."

"I remember a gypsy saying the same thing."

"She liked you. But there was no more she could do."

"Who are you?"

"Whoever you want me to be. Am I as beautiful as the gypsy?"

"You are more beautiful."

"Yes, I am. I am. I'm like the anemone on a reef, at my fullest when the tide is in. Don't you think so? Will you forgive me like you forgave the gypsy?"

Before he could answer she undressed and plunged into the water. The currents embraced her in a glimmering cocoon, and her body glistened. She dove then rose gleaming, and lay on the sand, spent and heaving. Her breasts glowed like silver fruit in the moonlight.

A crab's claw lay on the sand. She put it to her skin and scratched until the blood came, then tossed it away.

"Do you want me?" Her voice was silky and warm as it reached him.

Her face hovered above him, and he felt the weight of her body. A shudder ran through his muscles. He held her eyes unable to turn away.

"Do you want me as much as you wanted the gypsy?" she paused. "Do you?"

He nodded.

She tossed her head back with a soft laugh.

"You must do what the others did and see what lies beyond the reef, what secret lies hidden there and bring it to me. Then we can lie together forever. Nothing else will matter. You will have found the paradise you seek, and you will no longer be an outsider."

He rose to his feet and undressed then entered the water feeling a clarity he'd never known before. The lights of a ship loomed ahead as the smell of gardenias drifted over him from land. The last sound he heard was the gray-eyed woman's soft laugh.

A View of Toledo

WHEN SHE ASKED HIM about the blueberries, several shoppers stared at him and then at her, wondering at their relationship. He made a mental note to remind her again of how to behave when she was with him in public.

It would be impossible to leave the local farmer's market without drawing further attention to himself. He had no choice but to watch her study the blueberries, select a carton, place it in her shopping cart, and then stride away.

He didn't believe she said the words about the blueberries intentionally. She wouldn't. Everything she said had that same matter-of-fact quality, whether she was ironing his shirts or preparing a meal. Ironing's done, Ash. Meal's done, Ash, emphasizing the *Ash* even though his name was Ashton.

He remembered the first time they'd met when she'd rounded a street corner in the old part of Springfield where he lived and bumped into him. "Watch it there, Mister," she had said. The sound of her husky voice had made him want to bump into her again. She was someone who could be assertive, yet not unpleasant. A change from what he expected a stranger to say.

"Well…" she said.

"Yes…" he answered.

"Do you like fruit?"

"I never considered it."

"You should. I'm on my way to get fresh strawberries. They're great here."

"I'll remember that."

"See you do."

She was six feet tall and attractive with long blonde hair and almond-shaped eyes. He'd never bumped into a woman as tall before. The sensation was one he wanted to enjoy.

She was an excellent cook, graceful as a ballet dancer in bed and sometimes an erratic driver who liked to point out the passing sights. He knew she'd never leave him for an unpublished poet as Solange had. That wasn't her way. He'd even put off his latest travel plans to the coast of Albania to be with her so he could plan their trip to Toledo, Spain.

Two days after their accidental meeting, they met again, passing each other on the sidewalk. They each nodded.

"Are you doing anything tomorrow night?" she asked.

He'd accepted her invitation and found her receptive to his presence. Her friends felt their initial meeting portended well for the future.

He was ecstatic that at last, he'd found someone, who in his eyes, could do no wrong. And besides, she always smelled nice and fresh, much different from the muskiness of the foreign women he'd met on his travels.

She liked to introduce him to her friends by using his full name, Ashton James Watson, then added famous world traveler.

"It's an ancient name," she said to anyone who listened. "I envy your history, Ash. My family is commonplace compared to yours. I want to take you home to meet my family," she said to him one day while they sipped white wine at a café overlooking the Branch river that ran though Springfield. "I think they'd like you. My father always dreamed of traveling. I have too. There are just so many intriguing places: Tangiers, Hong Kong, Malaysia, Singapore, and Spain.

"You were right. This is the best place to enjoy wine. The best way. This café has a certain ambiance I like."

She drew out the sound of the last word so it sounded like aaammbeeance. Pleased with her pronunciation, she sat back and took a deep breath, eyes surveying the river.

"Don't you love it, Ash? I never realized how beautiful a river could be. Do you have a favorite one?"

At that moment, he didn't care about rivers; he only wanted to gaze at her and how the light fell on her like a translucent shield. Despite himself, he was genuinely in love with her for that one intense moment, a moment he would never forget.

"I've put you in my journal. Do you mind?" she said with an inquisitive frown.

He remembered she said the words with the same authority as when she'd asked him to put out mouse-traps, quizzing him later on whether a mouse had been trapped, or the lids on the trashcans were tight.

"Not at all. I've never been in a journal before."

"A first for you, is it?" she said in a playful voice.

"I've been the subject of gossip, but never written about in a journal."

"I see how that might happen," she said with a smile. "Was the gossip true?"

"I hope so. "

"Did you have a reputation?"

"I like to believe so."

"Good for you. Did you have a special lover?"

"I might have."

"What was her name? I want to find out more about you."

If he answered he felt as if he would give up a piece of his life. For a moment he was silent. Her stare made him uneasy as he struggled for the answer he needed to provide.

"Her name was Solange. I met her in Tangiers. She left me for a no talent poet named Raoul."

"An intriguing name. I'm sorry about what happened. I hope you got good and drunk."

"I did, and I soon forgot her. So I guess it wasn't meant to be."

"I had a lover too, I guess. Like the best of loves, our affair was so brief it couldn't tarnish, which was for the best. We've seen each other twice since then. Time enough to reminisce, but not enough for things to become serious."

She grabbed his hand and squeezed it.

One month later when she suggested they move into his townhouse together; the decision had been easy.

◆

"Do you know there are many *Views of Toledo* by El Greco, Ash?" she asked him three days after she had moved in as they sat on his balcony drinking coffee. "Someone told me that after I'd spent a whole morning studying the picture at the Metropolitan Museum in New York. The whole experience seemed so cheap somehow."

"I see how it would," he said.

"I can't wait. Just the two of us, incognito, having coffee in an out-of-the-way cafe in Toledo. At last, I'll be able to figure out this El Greco thing for myself. Haven't you ever wanted to find an answer to one of those big questions of life?"

"I never thought about it."

"You need to, Ash."

He let his gaze shift from the finished crossword to the flower garden below. The body of a swallow lay on its back in between the yellow irises.

"It was the only painting I ever liked. Domenicos Theotocopoulos. El Greco," she said as she put her cup down on the edge of the table. "I remember the name from an art history course. It was just a slide, Ash, but I never forgot it. Then I found it in the museum."

Her voice trailed off as she watched a three-legged dog hobble across the lawn with something white in its mouth. The dog dropped it and tore it apart.

"Oh, God," she said. "That's my tampon. He's been into the trash again. Do something."

He laughed.

She shouted at the dog and reached for the nearest ashtray, stood and threw it at the animal. The glass shattered on the walkway below. The dog dropped the tampon and disappeared into the bushes.

"What did you do that for?" he asked.

"It's disgusting. Look at the lawn."

"I'll clean it up. There'll be nothing to worry about. No one will see your true blood. Dogs do things like that. In Europe—"

"Fuck you, Ash. I told you always to check the trash cans."

She sat down not looking at him.

"You can be such a prick, Ash. A real prick. I'm not sure I want to go to Spain with you."

"What about El Greco?"

The phone rang, and she rose to answer it.

"That must be Vivian," he said glancing at his watch. "She's late calling this morning."

She turned as if to speak, crossed the living room, and picked up the phone. Facing the wall, she paced in a semi-circle, her free hand twisting the cord.

He reached for the newspaper and opened it, pretending to read. By tilting his head down and to the left, he heard her words.

"Oh, yes. Really? I agree. It had to be. He's the usual. It's tempting. That would be fine. Bye." She put the phone down. "Lunch," she said. "Then the pool. I have to get ready."

"I thought you were going to play tennis with Rachel?"

"I changed my mind."

She loosened the belt of her robe, and it fell open. He put the newspaper down and followed her into the bedroom. She took the robe off went to the closet and reached for a yellow blouse and studied it. He came up behind her and slid his hands over her body. She pushed him away.

"When I was in the South Seas," he said. "I read about this love ceremony. The man takes the woman to a hut. Once inside, they sit facing each other and lock their legs in a crossed position. Then they touch foreheads and rock grinding together until blood runs. By that time, they are delirious, and they go down on the ground. Before they know it, they make love."

He looked outside again. The dog had picked up the rest of the tampon and was walking toward the bushes.

Crossing the Great Divide

A T LAST, he would show his wife and her therapist, Dr. Sloane, he'd had enough of being married. He and his wife, Angela, had reached that point in their nine-year marriage where nothing mattered anymore, and she had gained 30 pounds. The train trip had been hers and Dr. Sloane's idea to bring their family together and experience the country at the same time.

She sat next to her husband on the gray seat of the observation car. He smelled her breath mints and the exotic perfume he no longer found exciting. The diffused light of the observation car didn't compliment her.

At one end of the car, their son, Albert, pointed a toy pistol at a passenger.

"Bang," he said. "Bang. You're dead."

The elderly passenger scowled at the lanky seven-year-old who had big squinty eyes.

"Bang."

"Don't bother the other passengers, Albert," said his mother turning away from the window. "You're being a bad boy. And you know what happens to bad boys, don't you?"

"Bang."

"Albert," said his father. "Do as you're told."

"I don't want to." His father rose and took a step down the aisle.

"Give me the gun."

"No," said Albert and dashed away. "Bang. Bang."

His father lunged at him and caught his son's arm. Albert struggled as his father dragged him back to his seat and shoved him next to his mother.

"Now stay there." He clenched his jaw.

He returned to his seat across the aisle and stared at the passing landscape. Antelopes bounced away from the rush of the train. New Mexico with its bleak terrain, rugged black mountain ranges and lonely reaches filled him with new courage. For a moment he imagined himself with the antelopes, hooves thumping on the hard earth as he sped away toward a beckoning ridge covered with pine where something new awaited.

"Come see the antelope, Albert. Quick before they're gone," said his father.

"I want to watch wrestling. '*Hulkomania.*'"

"There's no TV here," said his mother.

"Why?"

"Trains don't have TV," said his father.

"I want to see wrestling."

"Now see what you've done," she said.

She shook her head twice in that way of hers. The discussion was over.

"I want to see Indians," said Albert in a whiny voice.

A pickup truck ran parallel with the tracks and then turned off at a bridge over a creek bed. A hand beckoned from an open window.

"I'm hungry," said Albert. "I want a hot dog."

"You've already had a doughnut," his mother said sharply. "You'll just have to wait until lunch."

"Can't."

"Would you like a candy bar, dear?"

"No. I want a hot dog."

"I've already told you," she said.

"Hot dog. Hot dog. Hot dog."

"Will you do something about him?" his father pounded his fist into the seat next to him.

"What?"

"Take him to the bathroom."

"What good would that do?"

"He could watch the toilet flush. I liked that when I was his age. Whoosh. Whoosh. I thought it was hilarious."

"Don't be disgusting."

"I'm not. That's the noise it makes. Whoosh."

"Would you like that, Albert, dear?"

"No."

Albert stood and pointed his pistol at the conductor who swept past him.

"Bang," said Albert as he took a step after the conductor.

"Don't do that, dear," she gave him a warning look.

"Why?" asked Albert.

"It's not nice."

"Bang."

"Let's play a game. Would you like that?" She dug into her purse and removed two travel cards with lists of sights to check off.

"I want a hot dog," said Albert with a pout.

She placed the cards back into her large purse among the candy bars, chewing gum, spare change, and pencils. He gazed past her to the wooden and cement buildings along the tracks.

"My stomach hurts," said Albert.

"That was from eating the doughnut. I told you you'd be sorry," his mother said with an admonishing tone in her voice.

"It hurts. It hurts."

"Here." She reached into her purse. "Suck on this peppermint."

"I want a hot dog."

"I thought your stomach hurt?"

"It's better now."

He grabbed the candy and popped it into his mouth.

"You'll spoil his appetite," his father said sharply.

"It's only nine o'clock."

"What else are you planning on giving him?"

"I'll give him whatever I want," she said.

"Good." Albert rattled the peppermint against his teeth.

"I won't forget this," she said.

"Suit yourself. We're approaching the Great Divide, Albert. Come see."

"I don't want to."

"You do as you're told," his father said.

"Don't be so hard on him. For once can't we enjoy ourselves on a trip? Dr. Sloane said it was important."

"Did he?"

She gave him one of her looks.

"Where is it?" asked Albert.

"What?"

"The Great Division."

"Divide," he said. "The Great Divide. We're crossing it now."

"I don't see it," said Albert.

"You can tell your friends all about when you get back."

"Are you trying to start something?" she said. "Because if you are...."

"Joey's going to Disney World," said Albert. "Is there a Great Division there?"

"Sometimes I don't know what got into you," she said.

"Play with me," said Albert to his father.

"Not now."

"Bang. Bang. Bang."

Albert dashed down the aisle and took cover behind an empty seat next to a white-haired woman.

"How are you today, little man?" said the woman.

"I want a hot dog," said Albert.

"With ketchup or mustard?" she asked.

"Ketchup. I like ketchup and honey."

"So do I."

"You do not."

"It makes you grow big and strong," said the woman.

"Albert, don't bother the woman," said his father. "Come back here."

"Bang," said Albert.

"You got me," said the woman. She slumped against the seat, arms dangling to the floor. Albert touched her hand. She straightened.

"Boo."

Albert shrieked and dashed back to his mother.

"What did I tell you?" His father slapped him.

Albert bawled.

"Now see what you've done," she said. "Come here dear. Daddy's being very bad. Let's kick him off the train. Would you like that?"

Albert nodded.

The train hurtled into a tunnel, drowning out the rest of her words.

Her face hardened in the reflection in the window the way it might be on a quiet pond before a stone shattered the surface. He wished he had a stone to throw at the image before him, shattering it forever.

The Calf

W ES HOPED the long drive through the cold
December rain would be worth it. The decision to see Nancy again hadn't been an easy one. It
had been almost a year since he'd seen her. He missed
her more than he thought and wondered if she felt the
same. He remembered how her hair smelled of jasmine
and how she liked to press against him like a frightened
animal. He felt a heaviness no amount of liquor could
erase. His first Christmas without her was something
he didn't want to face.

On the date of their one-year anniversary she'd
asked him if he truly loved her, he didn't know what
to say. In bed that night she'd turned away from him.
The next morning, she no longer looked at him.

The day he'd left the rain was sharp and cold. He
never was sure whether the tears were hers or the rain
on her cheeks.

"How could you ask me such a question?" He stood
by his car. His chest tight with desperation.

"Perhaps it was time."

"What is it that you want from me?" he asked.

"Don't you know?" She'd turned away when he tried to kiss her goodbye.

◆

He stopped his car in front of her farmhouse, shut the motor off and listened to the rain drum on the roof. Even with his thick coat, the night still felt cold. He reached across the seat, found the whiskey bottle he kept for such occasions, finished what was in it, then got out. She stood silhouetted in the doorway.

"Who is it? Who's there? Is that you, Doctor?"

She came down the steps toward him. The sharp beam of her flashlight caught his eyes and he turned his head away. The light snapped off.

"Merry Christmas," he said.

"You've been drinking," she gave him a disgusted look.

"I was cold."

"What do you want?" Her voice was beyond icy.

"I missed you."

Ground fog swirled around them.

For a moment he felt like leaving and stared down at the puddles of rain which formed around his feet.

"What do you want me to say?"

He turned up the collar of his coat, a sinking feeling in his stomach.

"I thought you were the vet. A cow's about to calf."

The fog obscured her expression.

"Since you're here, we better see how the cow's doing," she said. "She's the one who chased you."

"I was pretty scared, but you and your father thought it was funny."

"Someday she'll have a healthy calf, a prize bull. You wait and see."

He followed her to the barn and slid open the door. A splinter scratched his palm. The black and white cow stood over the inert calf, licking the body with her tongue. He knew the calf was dead. In the dark, the cow's eyes watched warily. The small brown body was nothing but legs; its pink tongue, caught between its lips, pointed upward as if ready for suckling.

She gave him a pair of rubber gloves. Without waiting, she grabbed the calf's feet. The cow butted her and then moved away. She dragged the body toward the open door. She stopped, dropped the calf, took a small pitchfork from the stall and turned the placenta over into the hay, then went outside and backed her pickup to the barn door. Wes lifted the calf into it. The night was icy black. He climbed into the truck. The cab was cold, and his breath clouded the window.

Nancy put the truck in gear and started down the road to the highway. Country music from the radio faded in and out. The scattered lights of other farmhouses glittered through the rain. They turned into a rutted road, bounced past an abandoned building and stopped in some weeds by a broken down well. She got out and opened the tailgate and watched while he slid the calf into the hole where it landed with a thump. She looked away, and he felt his stomach lurch. Windy puffs of rain slanted over the dirt road. The harsh lights of the truck silvered the building. She grabbed his hand and held it tightly. He suddenly felt like holding her—to touch her body and hear her heart race.

"How about something to eat?" she said. "You must be hungry. I have eggs, but I can still only scramble them."

"Your scrambled eggs were always pretty good."

"Bullshit," she said.

◆

Wes poked at the wood in the fireplace with a pair of tongs. The fire squeezed up between the logs with a fierce light.

She broke the eggs into a glass bowl, stirred them quickly with a wooden spoon and poured the mixture into a pan.

A crack of blood had dried across his palm where he'd scratched it. On a farm, blood was a sign of work—a sign that something had been accomplished, finished and talked about later over steaming coffee in a kitchen like Nancy's.

She scooped the eggs onto a plate, put them in front of him, and sat.

"I'm afraid as usual I've burned them a bit."

"That's all right. I don't mind."

Outside the rain fell over the dark still fields. He took a bite of the eggs, eating with a gusto that surprised him.

He finished and felt Nancy look at him. Not raising his eyes, he studied the contours and lifelines on his hands. They seemed to go nowhere.

She rose and took the empty plate to the sink, then came back and kissed him on the top of his head. He stiffened.

"To cheer me up the night after you left my father took me with him to Howard Johnson's. Every Saturday, when my mother was alive, the two of them went out. They saw a movie in town, then had a drink and ended up at the Howard Johnson's on Route 5 for something to eat, a turkey club for her and a tuna for him. They smelled of potato chips when they each kissed me good night. I thought there was more to life than ending up at Howard Johnson's. But I guess I was afraid to admit what I knew. It was as if they had been on their first date again and nothing else mattered."

He didn't want to hear any more. It made him feel uncomfortable. "It's stopped raining," he said.

"The streets in town will be like mirrors," she said. "You never know what's real and what isn't. By the time you figure it all out, it's too late."

"Remember our first date." He grasped at the memory. "We'd been caught in the rain. I'd seen rain before, but that day it had a different smell—your smell, fresh and sweet. And you were shivering like a frightened fawn."

"Don't," she said. "Don't."

"Aren't you lonely living here?"

"I was lonelier when I was with you. I know that now."

A fringe of the moon showed behind the clouds that hovered above them.

"It's going to clear," she said. "The moon is out. It will be a good day tomorrow."

A good day for what? He imagined himself sliding like that calf had, through a cold black dark. Tears spilled down his cheeks, tears he hoped would wipe away his memories.

The Blue Lady

COLONEL HIDALGO of the Ninth Regiment wasn't a drinking man, but today was different. It had been a day not to be forgotten, one he could recount over and over while sitting on the porch of his retirement villa in the mountains near the Central American town of San Nueva. He had executed Lopez, the rebel leader. It had been his duty, the duty of every loyal soldier. That was all. Just as Lopez's duty had been to resist him, his had been to capture the bandit and bring him to justice, whatever the cost.

After the execution, the Colonel had returned to the hotel near the railroad station to collect his bags before heading to the railroad station to wait for the train. His work was finished and promotion was imminent. His family would be proud.

From the window of the hotel the government oil rigs, thick as a forest, stretched west to the edge of the earth. The smell of oil and the odor of the peasants who worked the oil fields were something he could now forget. How could these people be so unclean? The notion made him shudder. The rigs and the oil workers, which he had been ordered to protect from

Lopez, reminded him of giant mantises, praying to their oil master.

On some days when it was too hot to breathe, the Colonel stayed in his headquarters, listening to the sand ping against the tin roof. Despite the heat, there had been the execution.

The Colonel hoped the train wouldn't be as late as it sometimes was. In his years as a soldier, he couldn't remember a train being on time. It was one of the few things the government had no control over. The large engines built in the 1930s broke down; the tracks buried by sand, flooded out, or were torn up by men like Lopez.

He found a seat in the deserted waiting room, and with time at last to reflect, from his tunic he removed the note that Lopez had sent him last Christmas. The boldness of the rebel leader always fascinated the Colonel. From the beginning, he suspected Lopez was very dangerous to the future of the government, and its oil fields which made the government rich.

Dear Colonel:

Since you and I are not acquainted, never having been able to get together and scrape up an introduction, I should still like to wish you a Merry Christmas despite everything between us. I am sure you do not lack clothes, and since I am uncertain as to your tastes in books and pictures, I can

only send you the ear of your captured lieutenant,
who allowed himself to think he had surrounded
me. So here is wishing you a loving and useful and
happy life and also that you may at least have a
very tiny tree at which to blink.

Your Faithful Servant,
Major Miguel Santiago Lopez

During the eleven years Lopez had been a rebel leader, he had never won a battle in the long struggle for the oil fields. The people of San Nueva had almost forgotten who he was. When the Colonel took a prisoner and marched him through the streets, he only encountered village dogs prowling for food. He wondered if it would be any different for Lopez.

For many years the government had ignored Lopez until one day an important man from one of the oil companies was discovered sitting in a large wooden chair in the center of the road. A large stick propped up his head. At his feet was a sign, which said:

WE DO NOT WAGE WAR AGAINST CIVILIANS ONLY ON THOSE WHO TAKE OUR LAND. WE WANT TO LIBER-ATE SAN NUEVA FROM THOSE WHO WANT TO IMPOSE THEIR WILL ON US. TO DO THAT WE MUST PASS THROUGH YOUR LAND. DO NOT PUT UP ANY ROAD-BLOCKS. LET US PASS. THIS IS AN EXAMPLE OF WHAT WILL HAPPEN TO THOSE WHO OPPOSE US. VIVA LOPEZ.

The rotting corpse brought the flies and with them the diseases they spread. The Colonel had been ordered to prevent further incidents in the territory; the government had enough problems already.

There was no one else. The younger officers were away on maneuvers in the West, and the others had yet to return from the North. At first, the colonel hadn't wanted to go, knowing what he would be facing. Then he changed his mind, accepting his fate, as Lopez accepted his. That was the way of life. And besides, orders must be carried out.

Many times during their years of battle, the Colonel came close to capturing Lopez, and as many times Lopez escaped. Once, disguised as a lady of great stature, he flirted with the Colonel who found him attractive. On another occasion, Lopez hid under the wide skirts of an old woman and escaped out a window into the night.

When Lopez was finally caught, he was in a filthy brothel near Rio Santos with a fat toothless woman under him. Because of their thrashings and cries, Lopez hadn't heard the Colonel approach and gave up without a struggle.

"We meet at last," said the Colonel.

"And there is nothing to drink," said Lopez with a slight bow of his head. "Next time we shall toast each other".

"By all means," said the Colonel with a sharp nod of his head.

Then turning from the Colonel, Lopez told the whore the seed he planted in her would continue the fight. She laughed and went to the stone basin to wash. "I don't want your child. It will put a curse on everyone by climbing into their shadows just as you have done."

Lopez' eyes glittered, and he struck her. The woman's laughter could be heard long after the house was out of sight.

In the search of Lopez' trousers, the Colonel found a tattered black notebook with writing in it.

1. Dinner. 1½ cup beans full of salt.
1 bread. Tea. Dirty cup, knife, fork.
The sores of children.

2. Supper. Strips of bread soaked in fat.
Little milk. Drought. Fields full of dust.
The women no longer sing.

3. Today. Oats. Very little oats.
The children no longer laugh.
Lots of milk. Stale bread. Coffee. Most
faint by 10am. No teeth. Gums worn out.
Boiled meat. Fit for dogs. My men are tired.

4. Tonight. Soup. No body to it.
3 pieces apple. 1 slice bread. Nothing
solid for their stomachs. Nothing solid.
Harvest is coming.

When the Colonel asked Lopez what the writing meant, he received no answer. After ordering Lopez be beaten, the Colonel sent the book to the government's intelligence office, noting that Lopez had his teeth, and children were laughing.

After his return to the village, the Colonel paraded Lopez down the main street. The villagers watched the moving procession. By the time the Colonel reached the jail, the street was empty.

On the first cool night after Lopez's capture, the Colonel went to visit him. The jail was an adobe hut with small windows; one outside wall was pockmarked with bullet holes. From the center of the airless room, a naked bulb cast a hot white light.

Lopez had been lying down, but rose when the Colonel approached. His face was swollen, and blood matted his hair above one ear. He held his broken left hand close to his side.

"Cigarette?" Lopez nodded, and the Colonel gave him one and lit it and put it between his cracked lips and puffed.

His eyes never left the Colonel who stood straight in the small cell.

"Are you being treated all right?"

"I wish I had a woman and something to drink," said Lopez.

"There is milk. Would you like that?"

"Yes."

The Colonel poured out a cup of milk from the pitcher on the table outside the cell. Lopez washed his hands with it.

"The milk is for drinking," said the Colonel

The Colonel was envious of the dirty little man who stood in front of him, and then he remembered who he was.

"If it had not been for the Blue Lady," said Lopez, "you would have had someone else to chase. When you see the clouds in the form of a lady in a flowing dress, she is nearby. It is her home. Blue flowers grow where she walks, and in her path blue birds follow. She always dresses in blue and brings luck to the good. For those who have seen her, the story is the same. If you reach out toward her, she is always out of reach. She has helped many.

"I was crossing the northern territories. It was many years ago when I was a young man of twenty. My canteen was dry. All day I walked in the hot sun searching for a spring. Darkness caught me because my pace was slow from the thirst. I still had hope, but the clouds moved in and hid the stars. I became lost in a trance and wandered most of the night. Just when I thought I was dead, the Blue Lady appeared and led me to the water. Because of that, I reached Lomas, where I raised an army, but it was harvest, and we did not fight that day. She will not come now because she helped me already, which is all any man is entitled to. I have searched many times for that spring, but it is not there.

It is for the others who will follow me to find. Now it shall save them. Our children must be free."

◆

The whistle of the train as it approached the station brought the Colonel out of his thoughts about Lopez and his execution. He looked forward to at last being free from San Nueva. He stood, picked up his bags and went out to the platform. No one got off, and the Colonel climbed into the last coach.

The train pulled away, beginning a ten-hour journey through the country to the capital.

A grizzled middle-aged man sat wedged between his two plump daughters. Stuffed into a threadbare blue suit, the sweating landowner, farmer or perhaps a small merchant—forced a nervous grin on the Colonel. Petit bourgeois fool, the Colonel concluded, smiling back. As stupid as his cattle or his customers, obviously one of the many Lopez had sought to free.

After rumbling through several tiny villages and crossing the brown waters of the Rio Tegria, the train stopped for no apparent reason other than to let a group of children approach the open windows. Little girls in tattered dresses and bare feet offered bunches of flowers. Boys stood behind them, waiting.

As if on cue, several of the train's passengers made a game of throwing pennies and candy out the windows, tossing the coins and candy further and further away from the children, watching them scramble and grovel.

It soon became tiring, and the passengers stopped yelling, waving their empty hands. The train moved again, the children running alongside.

As the Colonel turned to toss a coin, he glimpsed the stubby snout of a pistol held by one of the running children, heard a bang, then pitched forward, almost bending over double as the train jolted ahead, its horn bleating. Outside, he made out a graceful cloud skirting the horizon.

Birthday Boy

TODAY I'M THIRTY-FIVE YEARS OLD; last year I received another necktie I never wore from a distant cousin in Joplin, Missouri. A headache I had yesterday is still there. The seven aspirin I took an hour ago have done nothing, a dull pain presses on the back of my eyes.

The landlady's old pit bull terrier barks at an imaginary sound. Her husband, who died two years ago, was the apartment maintenance man. He had cataracts and arthritis had crippled his left hand. I came upon him once with his zipper undone in the basement where he was looking at a picture of a naked girl. He stared in my direction, unconcerned like he always was, then returned to the picture.

The whiskey I've saved for my birthday celebration has done its work, and I'm ready to face the streets again. Sometimes I'm out all night, other times I listen to my radio until dawn before I have to go to work. The hallway smells like someone has been sick. And the elevator is stuck again. I walk down the three flights of stairs to the sidewalk and then stand for a moment deciding what to do next.

It's snowing hard. The damp cold chills my feet through the thin soles of my shoes. I look up into the dark the snow stings my face. I descend the stairs into the chilly subway tunnel, which I imagine are the caves of our beginnings. I look for the cave paintings, but they aren't there, they never are, yet I still look. The Broadway Local screeches to a stop. I enter the last car and find a seat where I can look back to see where I've been. I watch a pale-looking girl with shoulder-length black hair elbow her way toward where I sit. She stands over me, bracing her thin body in the swaying car and studies her reflection in the roaring darkness of the tunnel the way I have done many times before. I see that her breasts are small and that she wears no makeup. I guess she is in her thirties, but I can't be sure because the city sometimes ages people faster than they expect.

The train lurches around a curve, the wheels flash blue lightning, and she stumbles against me. I slant my legs out of the way, and she gives me a wary look.

I close my eyes, wondering if her panties are thin enough to see the way it was with the woman I picked up the other night near Tenth Avenue.

I held them to the light and could see the light bulb on the ceiling through the thin white nylon. The room was warm and smelled of her lighter fluid. The woman was in the bathroom, and I could hear water running, then she came out and stared at me. Through the filmy material, her face was indistinct, dark like her sex had been. I was erect.

"Little late now, honey," she said. "You want to do it again; then you got to pay me more."

She laughed, crossed to the bed and grabbed her panties.

The train jerks to a stop. I open my eyes and see the girl push her way out into the station platform. I follow her. She stops and takes out a small mirror. I come up behind her. She isn't at all startled and seems to be expecting me to approach.

"I'm sorry," I say. She arches her eyebrows. "I'm sorry about our legs touching like that."

She closes her mirror. "That's all right," she says indifferently.

Her hair blows up about her face as an incoming train pushes a cold, clammy wind through the tunnel.

"It's the subway," she says. "It's always so hard to keep your balance when you're riding… Sometimes it's even difficult on the street with all those people rushing past you."

"Do you want to go for a drink?" I say. "It's my birthday."

"I've heard that one before."

"But it is. I'm thirty-five. No one should be alone for a birthday. My life is nearly half over. How many times do you get to celebrate someone's thirty-fifth birthday?"

She studies me. I feel uncomfortable in her stare.

"Where were you thinking of going?" she asks.

"I don't know. Anywhere. Off the streets. We can go to my place, maybe."

"I guess so," she says, shifting her eyes from mine. "Besides, it's early yet. I'm going to a party later for some people from Nevada."

"Nevada?"

"They moved to a place on East 91st."

"I live a few blocks away," I say. "We can walk if you don't mind the snow."

"It never snows for very long here," she says. "It's the heat from the buildings. Are you going to get something to drink? You can't have a birthday without something to drink. I have to get some cigarettes," she disappears up the stairs into an arcade.

I follow her and watch her put several coins into the machine, punch a button for filter tips and the cigarettes clunk out. She breaks the pack open and lights up.

Several men press about the glass-topped pinball machines at the back of the arcade. A couple dressed in leather jackets watch a man hit his machine. He swears.

"This way," I say. "I want to show you something."

I take her arm and lead her back to the Big Game Shooting Gallery. I put four quarters in the slot and slide my body behind the rifle. My eyes follow the lines of ducks, bears, and deer as they move through the painted scenery. I squeeze off the shots. The invisible bullets tumble the animals in a neat row.

She frowns.

"You try," I say. "It's easy."

My hand brushes over her breasts as I show her how to aim the rifle and slowly squeeze the trigger. Her hair catches in my mouth, and I brush it away, tasting a faint and bitter perfume. Her shots go wide, and the painted forest dims, the scoring light throbs bright pink.

"I'm afraid I wasn't any good," she says.

"When I was in the Army I wanted to be a sharp-shooter. Instead, I ended up in the Arctic where I collected information from weather balloons."

"I always liked balloons," she says.

We head back to the street. It has stopped snowing. She walks ahead of me. I stare at her legs.

"There's a liquor store around the next corner," she says.

The bright lights of the store hurt my eyes. I select a bottle of whiskey, pull out the bills from my wallet, and pay the clerk.

"Hey, how are you doing?" he says to the girl. "Haven't seen you in here in a while."

"I don't know what you're talking about." She takes the whiskey from me and goes back outside. He winks and gives me the change.

She's waiting for me when I come out.

"Who was that?"

"I don't know. He was mistaken. It happens all the time. How much further is it now?"

We turn another corner and stop in the center of the block. At the end of the street, a movie marquee flickers into the night.

A man in a bulky coat stands by the ticket booth looking at the snow. I go up the stone steps and unlock the outside door of the apartment building. The landlady's dog barks.

"The elevator doesn't work," I say. "I'm on the third floor."

I stare at her legs again as she walks up the stairs ahead of me.

I put the key in the door at the end of the hallway, turn the knob, and it opens. I switch on the light.

Cockroaches scatter across the floor and under the sink and red sofa by the window. I straighten the bed and toss a dirty shirt into a large cardboard box.

"It's cold," she says.

I bang on the riser until I hear the radiator sputter.

"Ever since my landlady's husband died things have been getting worse."

"Isn't that always the way?" she says. "How about a drink? Whiskey with Seven-Up if you have it."

I open the refrigerator and break open a tray of ice. I leave the ice tray in the sink, and run warm water over my hands until I feel myself stop shaking.

"It's not much of a place," I say.

"I've seen worse. You have any music?"

"Just a small radio."

I take the radio from the table near the bed. I turn it on and place it on the top of the bookcase next to the sofa. She sits, I mix our drinks and give her the glass.

"Here's to the birthday boy," she says and raises her glass in a toast.

I sit down next to her and touch her body with mine. She sips her drink and lets me put my arm around her shoulder.

"Do you work?" I ask.

"Only if I feel like it," she says. "Sometimes I model. Bikinis in December and fur coats in summer. What about you?"

"I work in the calendar section of a publishing house. I was lucky. I got out of the army and was hired right away because I was a veteran. I check the months for proper spelling. order, and color. Sometimes if there's a mistake, you can make a few extra dollars finding it. I've been there ten years now."

"That's too long," she says. "That's too long to stay at one thing. That's like being dead. How about freshening this up," she hands me her glass.

I get up and cross to the sink. I pour in the whiskey and Seven-Up.

"What's your name?"

"Janet," she says.

"I'm Tony."

"The first man I ever dated was named Tony. I don't remember how I first got to know him. It was one of those things, just like now."

"Want to dance?"

She shrugs.

She gets up, and I take her gently through a slow step. The song ends, and she stays in my arms looking at the silhouettes of two people on the shade across the alley. "Who are they?"

"I don't know. Sometimes the two of them fight and have their TV on too loud. Other times when the window is open I can hear them screwing."

She breaks away and sits on the bed, examining the unfinished crossword on the bedside table.

"Mind if I try to finish this? I knew a man who could do one of these in half an hour. He'd get on the train at New Brunswick; by the time the train had reached Newark he'd be done."

She sets her glass down and takes the radio from the bookcase and places it on the bed, folds the newspaper into a rectangle and lies back against the headboard. She puts the end of her pencil in her mouth and sucks on, knitting her eyebrows.

Her skirt rides up almost to her thighs, and I can see her underwear. She looks at me.

I pour myself another drink and watch her.

"Hey?" she says. "Don't take all the whiskey for yourself. Make me another, will you?"

I quickly down my drink, almost choking on it, then cross to the bed and sit down next to her and begin to fondle her breast.

She pushes me away and gets up.

I suddenly despise her.

"You know you're not bad looking," she says, "I'm sure you don't have to do things this way."

I say nothing and stare out across the alley. The shade has been pulled up, and I see nothing but the TV set.

I get up and turn away, my headache making me want to cry out. I go to the bathroom. I reach toward the mirror touching the reflection, then pull back, afraid. I splash water on my face, not wanting to return to the front room, but I don't know where else to go. I look out the small window and see the lights of the city shining through the snow, which is getting heavier and heavier. The door to my apartment closes.

In an apartment next to me a baby cries in a high pitched scream followed by whimpering, then silence. The baby cries again, this time it doesn't stop right away. The shrill cry rises then falls, then rises again giving way to an exhausted whimper that ends in an unworldly silence.

The Stars
Are Out In Cabland

I S IT SO MUCH TO ASK to catch a glimpse of the pure, clear stars against the sky? Will they still be there ten years from now in 1983? I can't help what I am. It just happened. When I gaze at the stars, I'm part of something beautiful and far away where nothing matters.

From the floor of the cab, I pick up the cheap western I wasted seventy-five cents on. The cover has a picture of a cowboy with his gun drawn.

I start with the blurb on the back cover. *'Revenge. Hate. Love. Roper came to Wells Crossing planning to marry pretty Barby Ann. He was fed up with the lawman's life. All he wanted was peace. But there was to be no peace in Wells Crossing as long as Luders was alive.'*

The park by the cab stand where I stop is empty. I tire of waiting for a fare and start the engine. The motor sputters and dies. As usual, the cab needs a tune-up, but what do the bosses care? I turn on the ignition. The engine coughs then rattles to life.

I drive past the building where Grace lives. The lights are off in her apartment. When I picked her up in the cab that first night, I never remembered seeing anyone so sad, a sadness almost as beautiful in the way stars are on the last deep black night of summer. It was that feeling that first made me call her.

"Stars?" she had said. "That's stupid. I'm not doing anything right now if you want to come up. I've never fucked a cab driver before, and I've got a bottle of whiskey. Maybe you're the one who can save me."

I'm never able to tell her my deepest feelings because it makes her mad. Every time I try, she stares out the bedroom window at nothing or goes into the other room. I need what she has, and I wonder if I love her only for that. Perhaps I should blame her for the screwed up life I live now because she doesn't care what I do. I wonder if someday I'll be able to ride out of the sunset in my cab and save her the way she wants. Then things might be different.

I pull up at the chili place on Broadway. The guy inside leans against the door, his thin, tattooed arms folded across a grease-spotted white apron.

"How's business?"

"Slow. Better on Friday. Weekends are always best. Friday, Saturday, sometimes Sunday." He nods his head to emphasize the last words. "You want anything? I can tell it's going to be a long night."

I go back to the cab as the dispatcher calls me and circle the square, heading toward a doctor's office.

There are still no lights on in Grace's apartment. Hopefully, she'll request me later like she sometimes does. Maybe I drive for the one crazy and innocent moment that made a difference like the night I met Grace. Other nights, it's a young sailor returning to his ship by midnight; a boy and girl on their first date at the movies; the girl in the green blouse with a kitten I bought milk for. The couple that argued, then kissed and argued again. The call is an old lady. I turn the cab around. She waits for me on the curb. I open the back door. She insists on sitting in the front seat. We say nothing. She leans against the door, turning her false teeth about in her mouth. She smells like a pumpkin. It's a three twenty-five trip. I get out and hold the door for her. She doesn't tip. I climb back in the cab. I hope she swallows her teeth.

The microphone fits in my hand. I feel angry at Grace for not being in her apartment. Why isn't she there? She has no place else to go. I click the button on and off.

"Who's doing that?" says the voice over the radio. "Who's doing that? I can't hear the other drivers."

I click the button again.

"Is that you, forty-five?"

"Three twenty-five," I say.

"Roger, forty-five."

I head back to the square. No other cabs are in sight. A new driver is lost. The dispatcher gives him directions.

"Where are you twenty-one? Where? The party just called. She can't see you. That's pretty good. Go back about ten miles. Nineteen, where are you? Get her. You know where the barn is, twenty-one? Good."

I get out and stand under a tree. Clouds block the stars. A park bum sits on a bench drinking beer from a bottle. He sees me and raises the bottle in a toast.

"Show a man a nickel, and he pays for his time," he says, laughing to himself, then rolls the empty bottle under the bench. He wanders off toward the harbor side bars.

"Forty-five?"

I head back to the cab.

"Forty-five?"

"Square," I say.

"The Toledo."

"Roger."

The Toledo's a rooming house near the railroad tracks. I park in front of it. I don't have long to wait. The guy goes to the Lightning Bar about this time every night.

"Forty-five. The Lightning."

"Roger, forty-five. Tell him to watch out for the pink elephants tonight."

"Fuck you," the man says to the radio as he gets in the cab.

The Lightning is seven blocks away. It's a quick silent trip. The guy gets out. He doesn't tip me.

"Fuck you, too," he says and slams the door. Loud polka music spills from the bar as he opens the door and goes inside.

I head back to the square. The street is quiet, and the cab lumbers along. I stop at the phone by the movie theater on the other side of the park.

"Forty-five. Three fifty. Out for a couple."

"Roger, forty-five. Bring me a couple, too."

I get out and dial Grace's number. No answer. No answer.

I slump back into the cab.

"Forty-five back."

"All right, back."

Outside the theater, a fat man stands with a child who is eating ice cream. The fat man keeps pulling a watch from his pocket and checking it.

"Gotta dime, Mister?"

A guy I didn't see coming shoves his head through the window before I can close it.

"No."

"Come on. You guys always have dimes. You can't fool me."

I give him a dime, hoping he'll go away.

"Thank you, Mister. Thank you for your help. You looked kind. Kindness is a good thing. I'm taking up a collection for the Savior. He's coming here soon. He'll need money to get started."

"Can't give any more. Later maybe."

"Yeah. Later."

He drifts towards the theater. The fat man grabs the boy's hand and pulls him away. I don't hang around to find out what happens and head back to the cab stand.

I pull over to the curb by the park and sit in silence, the buzz of Grace's unanswered phone echoes in my head.

The words on the back cover of the western make no sense. There is no way to escape. Someone always gets the girl and someone still gets hurt.

Windy watches me from his park bench. He's the one wino I like. He gets up, walks unsteadily to the cab and sticks his head in the window. The smell of liquor is strong.

"How you doin', Ace?"

"Workin', just like always," I say.

"Drivin' a cab ain't work. What I do is work. I'm the only guy in town who can get locked up, beat up, but I do get fucked up. Now that's work." He laughs, his old body shaking. "Seventy-years-old and need a drink to clear my eyes. Seventy years and going to run for dog catcher. Dogs like me. When I was on the chain gang, I escaped. I was found feeding the bloodhounds with hamburger. A dog catcher."

He totters off, laughing harder.

"Forty-five?"

"Square."

"A young lady at the Carlton."

"Roger."

When I arrive, I see that she is thin with dark hair and brown eyes and has a small suitcase which she doesn't let me take.

"I'm going to the train station" she says. "I have to get back to New York."

"Forty-five. Train station."

"Roger, forty-five. Be careful with that young lady now. . . ."

She looks at me. She doesn't seem pleased.

"That's just Lou."

"I don't care who it is. I should talk to his boss."

"It wouldn't do much good. The boss likes it."

"Well," she says. "In New York such a thing wouldn't happen."

I'm trying to get a good view of her in the rear view mirror, but she's sitting in the shadows.

I pull up in front of the station and she gets out. I hope the train is late, and then I could ask her if she can see the stars from where she lives. She doesn't tip me and slams the cab door.

"Forty-five. Five sixty."

"Roger, forty-five. How was she?"

"More than you could handle."

"Now, now, forty-five."

I breathe the girl's lingering perfume. The street lights at the curb are much too bright. What will I do tomorrow with Grace? One day I took her to the zoo because she said she liked animals. Another time we went to the beach to see a whale she'd read about which washed ashore, but it wasn't like she expected. The corpse had decomposed, and the smell was over-powering. We headed for the nearest bar.

I get out and phone again. No answer. No answer. I pick up the western once more and skim the words as my stomach tightens.

"Forty-five?"

"Bus."

"Big G Market."

"Roger."

I leave the book lying on the seat, knowing I'll never finish it tonight or any other night.

I pull out into the street and start for the Big G. It's a late shopper going home with food. I help her with her packages.

"Forty-five. State Street."

"Roger, forty-five. Don't get hungry."

The woman stares straight ahead for the whole ride. I hold the door open for her and help carry the bags into the building. She tips me a dollar. I walk back to the cab and sit.

"Forty-five?"

I don't feel like answering.

"Forty-five? Forty-five?"

"Four dollars."

"Roger, forty-five."

The door opens.

A drunken, heavy set man slides into the back seat. "The Spot Lite," he says. "That's the place I want to be. The place where everything happens in this fucking town. The people there will understand what I have to say. How stupid can we Americans get? We're fooling around with Russia and the Cold War and space exploration, getting poorer and poorer, spending money all wrong. Our enemies are laughing at us fools." He leans forward and pounds the top of the seat with his fists.

"We're so sure of everything when all the time Russia is getting ready to invade us using missiles and bombs. You watch. I know what I'm talking about. I'm telling the truth. Even here our enemies will get us. You think they care about you? No one does."

He motions me to stop, gets out and gives me a three-dollar tip, then heads into the strip joint.

"Forty-five. Three dollars."

"Roger, forty-five."

I roll down the window and stare at the sky, half expecting the enemy missiles to be there. The stars are shining through a hole in the clouds. I'm alive for another night.

I get out and try Grace once more.

"What?" she says.

"The stars are out."

"You're not into that again, are you? When you coming home? I got whiskey."

I stare at the sky, half expecting the enemy missiles to be there. The stars shine through a hole in clouds. I'm alive for another night. The whiskey can wait.

Laughter for a Padre

T HE DOCTOR EXPECTED THE PADRE at the birth of this child, first son to Ruiz the carpenter. A new birth pleased The Padre. Afterward, over tequila in the doctor's office, The Padre would talk about what he would do for the child, how he would baptize it and teach it the ways of God.

When the doctor slapped the child on the bottom, the baby cried lustily, and the doctor oiled him then wrapped the wriggling body in a blanket. As an afterthought, and because The Padre wasn't there, he popped garlic in the baby's blanket to keep evil away. He knew the child's mother would like the gesture.

The woman's labor had been hard, and there were signs of it in her face. This was a welcome child, unlike many he and The Padre had attended. The mother held out her arms and took the bundle.

A neighbor would be in after supper to help clean. The doctor lingered with the mother and child hoping The Padre might still arrive. "What's his name?" asked the doctor.

"Carlos Manuel Ortega," said the woman proudly. As good as any, the doctor thought. He hadn't had a

Carlos in months. He placed a cold cloth on the woman's forehead.

"Where's Ruiz?" the doctor said with a frown. "Why isn't he here?"

"He is getting drunk at the cantina with the gypsy. She said we would have a son. Where is The Padre, Doctor? I want him to bless my Carlos. He must bless my child. It is what I want done. I want to make my God happy. Why is The Padre not here? He was at the Gonzalez's for their son. Does he no longer love us?"

"I'm sure he does. I'll look for him."

Where had The Padre gone this time? Last week he'd come down from the mountains with feverish eyes speaking incoherently about salvation.

Before coming to Espiritu, the doctor had worked in the Canal Zone treating the Americans in service there. It was a job he never liked. There was more to medicine than taking temperatures and giving out pills to the rich; he needed a purpose for his skills and knowledge. He had jumped at the chance to work with a man dedicated to helping the poor who asked for little in return.

At first, it had been hard to adjust to the new life, but over the years the doctor had built up a toughness to the surrounding conditions, just as The Padre said he would or face failure.

The doctor put on his raincoat and stepped into the rain which was thick in the mountains, but in the street was only a thin gray haze that bore the pungent scent of mud and the peppery odors of food. A damp chill spread through the village.

As much as he hated the rain and what it brought with it, the misty countryside still excited him in the early mornings. The shifting of the sun and vapor were like the beginnings of a new world. Yet he knew it wasn't so.

To the west, around the dirt airstrip, a burnt-out plane lay where it had crashed. To the north was the cemetery where crude crosses tilted from the soil. Metal tags, made from the lids of cans, had been nailed to each cross. They glittered when the sun caught them before slipping behind the trees.

Maria, his housekeeper, and first patient met him as he came in from the rain. She helped him out of his coat and hung it in the hall. Age had been kind to her. When he first found her, she had been near death from malnutrition and infection. Her round face and dark eyes, bright with fever, reminded him of the sweet and naïve look of a child. He restored her health. To repay him, she had stayed as his housekeeper.

"You have a visitor. He is in the living room," she said. "It is The Padre."

At sixty-eight, The Padre still appeared youthful and alert, yet his black bird-like eyes seemed focused on something in the distance. The years of living in Espiritu had carved ever deeper web-like lines on his face.

The Padre thumbed through a photograph album filled with pictures of the village children. On some pages, the labels and whole photos had been torn out by the curious villagers who had taken the images home with them.

"I expected you at the birth," said the doctor. "Why weren't you there? It was a boy. The first for Ruiz. Carlos Manuel Ortega. The mother's doing fine. She asked for you. She thinks you no longer love the villagers."

"Perhaps she is right."

"How can you say that?"

"You still have much to learn, my friend. What does she or any of the other villagers know about the love of God? How many of them believe Christ died for their sins? There is still much darkness, and the poison of doubt rests in their souls."

The Padre stared at a pot of small-petaled red flowers in the doctor's window.

"You can make poison from those," said the doctor, noting The Padre's interest. "The plant is rare. I didn't think it would grow well here. One of the villagers gave it to me yesterday. He came from the interior."

"Poison?" The Padre frowned.

"It can kill in a few seconds and can also be an anesthesia."

"When that farmer, Miguel Santiago, poisoned himself," said The Padre with a sigh, "he came home from the fields and kissed his wife and children. When I found him, he was sitting under his favorite tree with his shoelaces untied. He had just started attending church and had asked me for a Bible, which I brought to him. I never knew his soul was so troubled."

"You need a drink, my friend." The doctor poured out two glasses of tequila and gave The Padre one. Then sat.

The Padre gazed into his glass.

"You do what you can," said the doctor. "Isn't that what you told me? You can't stop now because things aren't going the way they're meant to be." He raised his glass. "To the future."

The Padre looked away.

When the doctor arrived in Espiritu twenty-six years ago on a bus full of women, children, and chickens, the only person to meet him had been The Padre. From the bus, the doctor had his first view of the village from the bridge over the broad and shallow river and the large church that dominated the huts and narrow streets.

The stone bridge was the only bit of paved road within one hundred miles. It was flat and hard as a floor and one-eighth of a mile long. Below the bridge as he crossed was a horseman in traditional poncho and sombrero splashing across the river with a dog at his heels, driving a few cattle. Naked children splashed in the shallows where naked children had splashed since before the Conquest.

The Padre had been waiting for him on the Plaza that had been worn bare by pigs, heavy rain, and many feet. He had a bottle of tequila and together they finished it. As they neared the end of the bottle, The Padre stared at the doctor with sharp intent eyes and said: "You are new to this life and flushed with thoughts of being a doctor where few have been doctors before. You know nothing of the poverty, sickness, and fear that is here. Sometimes I am full of such doubt that I wonder about my abilities. I fear I can no longer heal the soul or spread God's word. Then I see a new face among my congregation and know all is not lost. The next week, the face has vanished. You have no choice but to go on because there is nothing else for you to do, and always there is the hope that a new face will stay."

"There has been much more rain this season than I remember," said the doctor. "It is not a good sign. There will be much flooding and destruction."

"It won't be enough to cleanse the poison among us." The Padre rose. "In your flowers, the seas, the earth, and the air. We are dying of a disease for which neither you nor I have a cure. It is all around you. Even in the vast and tangled jungle, there is poison in the toad, the snake, and even in man."

Dogs barked in the street. The doctor stood and opened the door.

A new wave of rain clouds formed over the dark and ragged mountains. Lightning reflected on the under-side of the clouds and glowed like a distant explosion.

A young couple spattered with mud walked up the path. The man was muscular and unshaven with deep set eyes. His free hand was around the limping woman's shoulder. She was wide-hipped with long black hair. The doctor felt The Padre behind him smelling as he always did of mothballs.

The couple stopped in front of the door. The woman put the canvas bag she carried on the ground and flexed her fingers. The man swung the battered suitcase from his head.

"May we have something to drink?" asked the man. "Water, perhaps. My wife is very thirsty. I am Gomez. My wife is Rosa."

"Come far?" the doctor asked.

"Sixty miles, maybe."

"You seem in a hurry."

"It is our baby," said Gomez. "He is ill. We left him and our little girls with my mother where it is safe. We have land in one of the new districts, but we are still clearing it. It is no place for children.

"We have been traveling five days. The road is in bad shape. We had to help push our bus many times and had to build a few log bridges. But the last washout was too much. We left the bus and walked."

"There's no traffic going your way, said the doctor. "And the road's out ahead too."

The woman bit her lip, close to despair. Tears glittered from the corners of her eyes as she fought to keep from crying.

"If it's any help, the bulldozers have been sent for," said the doctor. "The roads might be open tomorrow. Please come in. Stay for the night. There's plenty of food and drink. I have a few beds next door in my clinic. I can examine your wife's foot later."

"Thank you," said Gomez. The doctor poured out a glass of water and gave it to the man's wife. She took a long drink and then passed the glass to her husband. He took a sip then returned the glass to the doctor. They picked up their luggage and stepped into the hallway, then followed the doctor to the clinic that was divided into cubicles off a dark central corridor. In the cubicles were tables and rough-hewn bed frames with thin mattresses and clean white sheets. Mosquito nets hung above the beds.

"If you need anything," said the doctor. "I'll be right next door. The walls are very thin; you will not need to shout."

"We will be fine," said Gomez. "We will be fine. Thank you."

The doctor returned to the sitting room where he filled his glass with tequila and then sat rolling it between his hands. The Padre stood nearby staring out the window.

The woman cried from the next room.

"I should never have left our child," they heard her say. "Never. It was a bad thing."

"It is not your fault" said Gomez. "We did what we thought best. Do not worry. Everything will be all right. I love you."

"I am sorry," said the woman in a calm voice. "I have been silly. Tomorrow the road will be open like the doctor says, and perhaps in two or three days, we can go home again. Our baby will be well. When we arrive, everything will be all right. We must have faith."

"Yes," said Gomez. "We will never separate again. Things will be better. We will ask God for help and The Padre for his prayers. He looks like a good man."

The Padre poured a drink and downed it. His face became flushed, and his eyes shone. The doctor wondered how bad this seizure would be. As always, he'd let things take their course.

"A good man?" said The Padre. "How in such a place as this can I maintain the purity of His church on earth? How?" The Padre shouted out the last word. "He has forgotten us here in Espiritu."

Gomez stood behind his frightened wife who was in the hallway.

"It's nothing," said the doctor. "Sorry to have disturbed you. The rain makes him so."

Gomez nodded. The doctor poured another drink to steady himself and then sat watching The Padre.

The Padre opened his mouth wide, screwed up his eyes, and screamed "Oh Lord." The surprised doctor banged his knee against the table.

Maria stood in the kitchen doorway and shook her head at The Padre.

"Now see what you've done," the doctor said sharply. "You have disturbed our guests and brought Maria from the kitchen."

The Padre said nothing.

Maria shook her fists in the air and then returned to the kitchen where she rattled her pots and pans.

"Our guests have enough to worry about without your rantings," said the doctor.

"Thank you," said Gomez. "It is all right. Our Padre is the same when he is with God. Thank you. He took his wife's hand and led her back to the clinic.

"Oh Lord," said The Padre in a low voice as he fell to his knees. "Oh Lord."

"Once more," said the doctor, "and I'll have to give you a shot. Do you understand?"

He took The Padre by the shoulder and pulled him to his feet.

"I mean it this time."

"Oh Lord," said The Padre and pushed the doctor's hands away. "And oh yes, dear Jesu, today we have in our midst a new little lost lamb, Carlos, who is crying out for salvation, but by whom? Tell me Lord, who is to bless Carlos? Who will save his soul? And for whom? I can do no more."

The Padre breathed hard and swayed as he stood in the center of the room staring at the backs of his hands. He blinked his eyes as though he had just come in from the dark.

"Tomorrow," said the doctor. "First thing in the morning, you come see me."

"Yes," said The Padre, as if he were thinking about something else. "Tomorrow things will be better." Then he lurched bareheaded out into the rain.

The doctor wondered if The Padre would be all right. Perhaps he should have given him an injection.

That way he could have kept him here. Each season The Padre worsened. Soon there would be little the doctor could do.

The doctor remembered that an Indian from the village once said he'd never seen a sadder bunch of people than those who worshipped God. When The Padre wailed about something, the Indian felt like laughing because The Padre was trying to feel holy and full of the spirit and then would forget what God was like. The Indian thought God and The Padre might enjoy laughing, true laughter, more than the silly wailing over sins. Laughter was good for the soul.

The doctor turned back from the door, shut it, then filled his glass again. During the four months of rain, things always seemed to go badly. It was a time when villagers were together in the close quarters. A loud banging woke him from his thoughts.

"Doctor. Doctor. You must come." The voice rose with the increased pounding. "Doctor. Come quickly."

The doctor opened the door. Olivio, the church sexton, stood in front of him. His face slick with rain. "It is The Padre."

The look of primitive fright in the man's eyes made the doctor's stomach turn, and he cursed himself for not having kept The Padre with him. The doctor grabbed his raincoat, and medical bag then followed Olivio out into the rain toward the church. The Padre lay near the altar. In his hand was a small vial. His face had the sad peculiar expression of one in a drunken sleep.

"Mother of God," said Olivio. "When he drinks like this, he is like one who is dead."

"It is not drink," said the doctor. "He is dead."

They picked up the limp body and carried it to the small sleeping room, then lowered The Padre to the bed.

"I will miss him much." Tears flowed from Olivio's eyes.

"I, too," the doctor said in a trembling voice. "I, too."

The doctor picked up his medical bag and walked back to the clinic in the rain. He would have another drink, perhaps more, and contemplate The Padre's act of despair and the future.

Later, he would care for the injured foot of the woman returning to her children.